"These inspired short pieces turn words into flesh, as characters from the Gospels tell their stories. With humor and humanity, Neil Thorogood brings them to life before our eyes. These wonderful monologues, deeply faithful to the text and fed with both learning and imagination, open pages you thought you had closed. Whether read in private, or from the Sunday lectern, they will intrigue, move, and bless."

—SUSAN DURBER, president from Europe, World Council of Churches

"I knew of Neil Thorogood's gifts as a visual artist, but here he shows his skill in sketching word portraits of New Testament characters. Deft, scholarly, sensitive, and imaginative. These 'Ignatian' reimaginings of Gospel (and Epistle) scenes are laced with exegetical insights as well as spiritual provocations and delights."

—DOUG GAY, senior lecturer in practical theology, University of Glasgow

"Cedar, eucalyptus, and fir: simply by naming the wood in Jesus' hands, his world and mine become one. With the imagination of an artist, knowledge of a preacher, and sensitivity of a pastoral minister, Neil Thorogood has created a beautiful companion to biblical faith and ministerial leadership. Filling familiar stories with detail and bringing untold stories onto the page, these texts are unsettling and tender, spacious and generous—welcome thresholds to bible study, liturgy, and prayer."

—JANET GEAR, program coordinator for ministry vocation, United Church of Canada

"Neil Thorogood's creative gifts coupled with his Spirit-led imagination have resulted in a treasury of pieces that will be meaningful encouragement to pastors and anyone who leads in liturgy and worship. These imaginative reflections will also serve individuals, groups, and families as we together travel through the liturgical year."

—DAVID DETERS, spiritual director

"Neil Thorogood uses his rich artistic imagination to invite us into deeper reflection and conversation with the story of Jesus as experienced by key figures in the gospel narratives. Each of these accessible portraits of someone around Jesus opens up new devotional and homiletical meaning, for pastoral leaders and lay people alike."

—JESSE ZINK, principal, Montreal Diocesan Theological College

Gospel Voices

Gospel Voices

Forty New Testament Characters Telling Their Stories

NEIL THOROGOOD

Foreword by Anna Carter Florence

RESOURCE *Publications* · Eugene, Oregon

GOSPEL VOICES
Forty New Testament Characters Telling Their Stories

Resource Publications
An Imprint of Wipf and Stock Publishers
199 W. 8th Ave., Suite 3
Eugene, OR 97401

www.wipfandstock.com

PAPERBACK ISBN: 978-1-6667-7962-2
HARDCOVER ISBN: 978-1-6667-7963-9
EBOOK ISBN: 978-1-6667-7964-6

VERSION NUMBER 11/15/23

To the congregations of Thornbury United Reformed Church and Trinity-Henleaze United Reformed Church (Bristol), UK. You were the first to hear some of these in worship. I will always be grateful for the ministry we share and for your wonderful encouragement.

The church is God saying: "I'm throwing a banquet, and all these mismatched, messed-up people are invited. Here, have some wine."

—RACHEL HELD EVANS, *Searching for Sunday: Loving, Leaving, and Finding the Church*

Contents

5: Holy Week

6: Easter

7: Pentecost

8: Following Jesus on the Way

Foreword

A GOOD STORY ALWAYS leaves us wanting more. And the story of Jesus of Nazareth, the son of God, is no exception: four rounds later, after Matthew, Mark, Luke, and John have each had their turn telling their own version of it, we're still left wanting more. More details. More clarity. More chapters (and while we're at it, a sequel too, please). We'd like the writers to give us a closer look behind the scenes at what the disciples were really thinking. We'd like a few more fleshed-out characters, and some answers to the questions that, in our opinion, were never properly addressed. And obviously we'd like to know what happens next, since good stories never end; they just hit pause, for a bit. When the time is right, they continue—and live on, through us.

This book is a shining example of that. What Neil Thorogood has done in Gospel Voices: Forty New Testament Characters Telling Their Stories, is to take us back to Palestine in the time of Jesus and pick up the story at some key junctures. Through his beautiful, imaginative retellings, we go straight to those "wanting more" places, each of which results in some deep, midrashic listening. We hear, for instance, from Joseph, Jesus' father, about how he fell in love with Mary, the most spirited young woman in the village. We observe King Herod, as he rationalizes his murderous orders against the children of Bethlehem. We meet Jesus' cousin, John the Baptizer, and then his little sister, a grown-up disciple; Judas Iscariot, who betrayed him, and Simon of Cyrene, who carried his cross; Mary, who held his dead body, and Joseph of Arimathea, who offered a tomb. We listen to some of the women Jesus healed and the men he taught as they relate their own encounters with the man they called Lord and Rabbi. And we join Thorogood on the margins of the gospel story, as we imagine characters who were never explicitly named, but surely were there to witness these wondrous events: the innkeeper's wife who helped deliver Jesus; a woman who was present at the Last Supper; a disciple sent to share the good news after Pentecost; a pilgrim in Jerusalem. As we hear from each person, we see how their stories intersect—and then how they intersect ours. We become witnesses. They were there, and so were we.

The organization of the book is ingenious. It follows the liturgical calendar so we can trace the story of Jesus the Christ through the Christian Year. We begin in Advent with Zechariah and Elizabeth, and continue through the Christmas season, with a shepherd in Bethlehem and Anna in the temple. We walk alongside Jesus through his ministry leading up to Holy Week, and transition to the Easter season and its culminating day of Pentecost. Along the way, forty different characters—a mix of women and men, young and old, known and as-yet unimagined—keep our journey one of discovery. No matter how many times you've heard these Gospel stories, you'll hear them afresh with Thorogood as your guide. You'll find spiritual wisdom, too, and ideas for small group Bible study and your own prayer life, as you read.

In the end, it's Thorogood's decision to write these stories from the point of view of each character that makes this book a treasure. The early church placed great value on eyewitness accounts. The Gospels have a historical component to them; the writers are keen to remind us that these events happened. Yet they also created something different, in the Gospel genre: a new focus on evangelical witness, as the narration of each witness is fused with confession, sealing the life of the witness to the testimony itself. The New Testament isn't simply a report. It's an announcement. It's a proclamation of good news for all of God's creation. Thorogood's Gospel Voices invites us to reimagine that good news for our own time and contexts, as we consider with joy what our own witness might be.

Anna Carter Florence
Peter Marshall Professor of Preaching
Columbia Theological Seminary
Decatur, Georgia, USA
October 2023

Acknowledgments

MANY PEOPLE HAVE HELPED bring this book into being. There are those who had a kind word after a few of these pieces were used in worship for the first time. Their comments and suggestions spurred me to write more and to begin to wonder if a book might be possible. I am very grateful to Matt Wimer and the whole team at Wipf and Stock for seeing the possibilities and giving this book the chance to become a reality. Your commitment and guidance have been an education. Edith Summerhayes brought her copyediting skills to bear on the original manuscript. Thank you for your amazing eye for detail, boundless enthusiasm, and thoughtful suggestions that enhanced the whole book. I am hugely grateful to Anna Carter Florence for her readiness to prepare a foreword. You have taught me much across the years, and it is a delight to have you reflect upon these words of mine. Jenny, Samuel, and Thomas have supported this whole journey and I can never put into words all that your love and trust mean to me. My father, Bernard, never lived to see this published. But his own writing and witness have shaped my life and ministry and, I hope, find some echo in these imagined characters. We miss you, dad.

This book has deep roots in the Bible and in God's people gathering for worship to break open, and be blessed by, God's word. More specifically, it plays with possibilities surrounding the people whose lives were first touched by Jesus. These pages, and my life, would not be as they are without him. His gift of life made new has been the heart of ministry for me. I hope this book can be an offering of thanks.

Introduction

WHAT THIS BOOK IS

HERE ARE FORTY SHORT monologues giving voice to characters we encounter in the four gospels and in the book of Acts. Some of these are people whose names we know: King Herod the Great, Simon Peter, Pilate's wife, Mary Magdalene, Cornelius. Others are imagined from the hidden background of the biblical story. You'll find people who were in Jerusalem during the festivals of Passover and Pentecost. There are people who were in the crowds listening to John the Baptist or as Jesus told a parable. They are a whole bundle of individuals whose stories I have made up, but whose stories have, I hope, plausible roots in what we read in our Bible. Some sit much closer to a biblical text whilst others start from a passage but then head in directions that are all mine.

In every case, starting with a biblical text felt important. As a working preacher, I have the privilege of making weekly journeys of discovery with the Bible and communities of God's people. We want to listen to this word that can challenge and bless, encourage and daunt, train and puzzle in equal measure. We travel with it in the expectation that the Spirit of God will work within and between the words written, the words read, the words preached and the words mulled long after. Often, my experience has been, gloriously unexpected things happen when the Bible is opened. We are encountered and seen and feel our contexts illuminated by words written thousands of years ago as if they were penned just for us in our time and place. We are grateful. And, sometimes, we are shocked and deeply challenged by the word we hear and find ourselves sharing.

Sunday by Sunday, the congregations I serve tend to follow the biblical texts laid out in the Revised Common Lectionary, widely used across denominations and around the world. I am a lectionary-based preacher. So, each of these monologues began its life with one or more of the texts found in this lectionary. They are arranged in a rough progression to coincide with the church's year, from Advent to Pentecost and beyond. To help you find particular pieces that might fit specific acts of worship there are biblical and liturgical indexes at the end of the book.

In each piece, I have tried to imagine myself into the experience of one person whose life we glimpse in the New Testament. I have tried to honor their context and situation. I have attempted to make them feel like real people, sharing their own experiences and emotions. But all of them are acts of imagination and, I'm sure, reflect much of me as their creator. Perhaps there is an echo here of ways of reflecting upon the Bible that encourage us to use our imaginations so that we can enter more fully into the events and encounters. We might be familiar with some of the spiritual exercises of Ignatius of Loyola (born 1491) in which we contemplate a passage by placing ourselves within it as the action unfolds. For generations, such exercises have unveiled new depths of meaning within the texts that can be so familiar.

I am also an artist and make much use of the visual within worship. These monologues have some things in common with the biblical paintings and sculptures that we may be familiar with. Just as artists across the centuries and around the world have sought to turn texts into something we can see, and thus brought the words to life in fresh ways, so I hope these pieces might let us find further treasure in God's word.

WHAT THIS BOOK IS NOT

This is not a book written by a biblical scholar. It is a book written by someone who regularly creates and leads worship, who preaches, and who tries to help and encourage others to find their own voice and place within worshipping communities. I am privileged to be a minister of the United Reformed Church in the UK. Since my ordination in 1992, I have preached from the Bible and helped God's people gather around that word as we sing and pray, read and listen, break bread and share wine, celebrate, grieve, and continue to live faithfully to be a blessing in God's world.

I am blessed to know, and name as friends, some whose vocation is in the academy. In their researching, writing, and teaching on the Bible and theology they open up to us more and more of the treasures God has for us to discover. Some of their work forms the background out of which I have written my stories just as it has informed and refined my sermons. But these stories are written primarily to add to worship by one whose vocation is to help shape worship.

HOW THIS BOOK MIGHT BE USED

As a resource for public worship, these monologues could sit well alongside a reading from Scripture of a text that informed their writing. They have their origins in services in which we wanted to find some fresh ways into the biblical material. They can amplify an element of the biblical narrative or invite questions arising from it. Sometimes, they offer a rather different way into a familiar passage, or suggest something we might not usually notice. They tend to invite a time of reflection, a chance to let the Bible sink a little deeper into our hearts and minds. We have often let them lead into a period of silence or a piece of music that helps continue the opportunity to let God's word speak.

I know how important a good index is for any worship resource! I've known the frustration of not being able to find, or remember, a great piece for a service because the book didn't let me find it again. To help, we've included two indexes at the end of this one. The first index offers the original biblical references from which these monologues started their lives. Sometimes, this is simply one biblical text. For other pieces there are several texts that overlap and that have informed what I played with. The second index sets these monologues within the liturgical calendar, showing which seasons and times of worship each piece originates with and thus complements.

There are forty monologues here for a reason. I was aware that another possibility for using this book was personal devotion and quiet times. It might be a helpful resource to use on a daily basis in Lent, for example. The pieces could be read in their order, building upon each other to add to our own journey with Jesus. They could become part of a regular Bible study or prayer group.

My hope is that this book might become useful in ways I can't even imagine. Perhaps there are pieces here that could be useful in opening or closing devotions for meetings and gatherings. It might be that you use them as evangelistic resources for presentations on the streets as much as in our sanctuaries. Maybe there is something here that invites your own writing, painting, and all sorts of creativity. That would be awesome!

Whatever ways this book works for you and for others, let it take us even deeper into the life, death, and resurrection of the one who told the best stories.

1

Advent

Zechariah, the Father of John the Baptist

GOD TOOK MY WORDS away.

It happened late in my life.

I felt settled in my faith and knew what I believed. I was glad to be one of the priests of Abijah. Elizabeth and I cherished the traditions of our people and knew the Scriptures. You could say that we had a bit of status as a couple amongst the elders. People turned to us for advice. We cherished each other. When you live decades with someone you get to feel comfortable in the ways love and home have shaped the world around you both. There was sadness too. Few people escape loss, and we knew our share. We had wanted children. We were disappointed.

That time I was in Jerusalem with my division. The Temple was another home to me. I was as familiar with its courts and colonnades, its rooms and its rituals, as I was with the rooms and ways of my own house. Elizabeth had sent me on my way and everything was as expected. We saw to the sacrifices and helped people bring their offerings. The smell of the incense and the noise of the pilgrims and the animals filled each day. We were always deeply aware of the awesome and terrible responsibilities we carried as we led the people in worship. We were as close to God as anyone could be, anywhere. That demanded pure hearts and minds. The washing and the prayers, our devoted obedience, made possible our calling and our serving.

At the heart of the whole complex, at the top of the staircase, was the sanctuary. Within was the Holy of Holies. Here, behind the veil that hung across it, was the Ark of the Covenant with its golden cherubim and its ancient stones. The seven-branched candlestick burned to shed a flickering light across the walls. This was God's footstool, the holiest place of all. To enter into such space was always to tread into mystery and majesty. We cast lots to let God choose who might burn the incense at the golden altar so that the prayers of the people might rise to heaven. To be chosen in this

3

way was the highest possible honor, the greatest responsibility. You could only ever be chosen to burn the incense once in your life. So, it made me breathless when the lot fell to me.

Leaving everyone else waiting for my blessing in the courtyard, I made my way inside. The smoke curled up from the coals into the shadows high above. I spoke the sacred words. And then I saw the angel. He was standing to the right of the altar, the flickering light playing upon him, his shadow stretching upwards until it was lost in the darkness.

Terror took me! No purification could fit me for such a meeting. No prayers could make me worthy. No faithfulness could stand before such a messenger. Who was I, with my weakness and my story, to be in such a moment?

But I was known; my soul was seen.

"Do not be afraid, Zechariah, for your prayer has been heard."[1]

What prayer? Some prayer for someone in the conversations of the day, maybe? My worries for our people? The longings for freedom that we carry so deep and hardly dare to name? Thankfulness or sorrow? What prayer of so many? What test was this?

The future began for me and for Elizabeth in that moment. A child! A boy! A gift from God whom God was naming with a name to take him out of the ordinary. A vocation woven from that moment; to be a messenger of all that God intends. His the task of preparation, opening minds and hearts to be ready to receive the Savior we have yearned to meet. His calling to make the story of salvation take root amongst us.

"To make ready a people prepared for the Lord."

All of this rolled and thundered as I struggled to take it in. Hardly thinking, I blurted out the obvious: we were too old, too tired, too used up. Elizabeth and I could not be part of such a miracle. And that was when my silence began. My voice and my hearing slipped away.

Outside, as the sun shone on the city so steeped in story, I had no words. My gestures and my face told everyone enough for them to know a vision had visited. But the details hid away in the spaces where the words should have been. I returned home, silent still. Elizabeth came through the shock of my arrival to face an even greater one. I had to write it down. My scribbles gave her the terrifying, unbelievable, impossible, beautiful answer to her deepest longing. We wept together. Then we slept together.

---

1. Luke 1:13a

She told me, later, of the power of God at work within. People rejoiced at the news of her pregnancy although they also wondered at the strangeness of it all. For fear of complications, we kept her close in the confines of our home the long months that stretched ahead. Dear friends and family kept eyes upon us.

I remember Mary's arrival most of all. Her story was known to us. It was the obvious companion to our own impossible situation. The old woman and the young girl. The miracles unfolding in their wombs. The hopes and the fears. The wonder of it and the terror of it. I saw Elizabeth dancing and imagined their singing as they clung to one another. Only they could truly know what it meant to be caught up in the risk and glory God was shaping.

On we waited.

Then the time came. I was ushered away as the women crowded close. I tried to imagine the pain and felt the fear. The promises of the angel kept ringing in my mind as I worried for my wife and longed for her safety. Faith can falter at such a time. But all was well. Taken in, there was my dear Elizabeth and, in her arms, the boy.

On the eighth day the time came for the circumcision. Everyone assumed that he would be another Zechariah. But Elizabeth spoke up, "No! He is to be called John." This was strange. We had no one named John in the lines of our families. They turned to me and signed for me to write what name I wanted. Taking the tablet, I wrote as my wife had said, "His name is John."

It was then that God gave me back my words. My ears were open to the sounds of our John as he cried in Elizabeth's arms. And now it was my turn to sing.

Elizabeth, the Mother of John the Baptist

MARY HAS GONE HOME now. Three months on and both of us carrying the weight as our babies grow. It is good that she has some company on the road across the hills; not a place to be alone in the night. She'll be glad to get back to Nazareth. We'll be waiting for her news when her time comes just as much as she'll be waiting to hear from us.

Not that we've been short of news! And not that people have been short of stories to tell about us. We are the impossible parents, the couple caught by God. I can just imagine some of the gossip! Probably best that I've not been around to hear it. Although even my seclusion in this house for these eight months will have fueled the wilder stories.

It will be soon that our son will be born. I can hardly believe that I have barely stepped outside for such a long time. But it has been for the best. He is such a precious gift that I carry, and we knew we had to take as much care as we could right from the start. The sickness was the worst of it at first. There were the aches and pains as this old body made room for new life. Oh, his kicking in the night! The sleeplessness and the tiredness. I have never been so tired.

Soon now. Bring him safely, please God!

Zechariah still can't speak. At first, to my shame, I rather enjoyed it. He's a good man and a faithful husband. But he has become a bit bossier as the years have passed. When he returned from Temple service without his voice, I was able to get on and do without his suggestions. But the frustration he was enduring quickly cured me. And when the evidence was clear that I was pregnant, when everything the angel said was coming true, we clung to one another and wept and I spoke the words to soothe us both. We have made it work with all the sign language. And the silence of our home has seemed apt for the miracle we are hosting. I imagine this must be one of the most prayed for and prayerful places in the land.

Mary's arrival has blessed us beyond imagining.

When we heard that she was on her way, and that she, too, carried a child for God, we could not wait. Zechariah would often sit by the village gate to watch the road. I made her bed ready for her and replaced the flowers from the field several times before, at last, she reached us. Zechariah brought her in, beaming. I held her close, and we both laughed as our bellies bumped into each other.

And that was when I felt him do much more than his usual kick. It was as if my unborn son was dancing! I staggered and Mary's smile vanished. Zechariah put his arm around me, protective, his face showing his concern. The tears came then. And I felt a strength begin in me, a joy so deep it made me gasp. I knew in that moment that our children belonged together. They completed each other as Mary completed me; the young girl and the old woman singing the songs of God. We were blessed beyond imagining. I spoke the blessing, made it real by giving it voice. Here I was, the ancient wife of an old priest, telling this young mother that she was carrying the Lord of all!

Zechariah lit the lamps and we settled in to eat. The talk was all about motherhood of course. Zechariah could only play the audience. I told Mary our story. I told her of the shock and how the news felt terrifying at first. Then Mary told us her story. It was as incredible as our own. There was the stormy fear and wonder in it, just as we had felt.

At the end, Mary looked into the fire and fell silent. The flames reflected in her eyes, dancing there. She took my hand as the silence grew. The enormity of these things and our futures filled our home. These works of God, these choices made, these lives entrusted! How to find the words . . .

Softly then, Mary started to sing.

She sang a song of thankfulness and praise. It was her testimony, her witness to the work of the God of wonders. She sang of who she was and who she had become because the hand of the Almighty had touched her. She sang of being chosen. She sang of life made within her and of her place in the story of God's people. Mary's song rose and her voice gained more and more strength as she sang of God's abiding, of faithfulness revealed across the generations, of God's sustaining power. She sang of lowly people lifted high. She saw the mighty and the strong made meek, the proud undone, the rich and overfed sent hungry away. She was seeing visions and they soared! The ancient promises were coming true, the poor and broken were being redeemed. Blessing and honor and glory and power were coming to those whose faith was sure. Our long despair was ending. Our exile was over. God was here. All was changed already, made new, reborn even as the baby in her waited. She sang of herself and of us all. She sang of hopes to shake the world.

By the time she fell silent, sweet Mary was on her feet and I was standing too, clapping and stamping and weeping. Zechariah was beside me, joining in despite his silence. This girl!

We needed the months then. They passed in endless conversation as Mary and I wondered about the times ahead. There was fear and uncertainty in it all. None of us knew how things would be. We knew that God was at work, and we wanted to play our part. But there were times when it all felt too big, times when we could not find the right words. Then we would sit in silence or Mary would go for a walk. Often, she would let Zechariah go with her and she would tell me afterward of the greetings from our neighbors and of all their questions.

It was on one of their walks that they first heard about the census. For us it was a bitter herb that tasted of captivity. It pressed home the truth of Roman power and promised us more taxes. But at least Zechariah and I lived where we were born. It would be so different and so hard for Mary and for Joseph. She faced the journey home to Nazareth only to have to make her way to Bethlehem. And all the time the baby would be close.

We knew she had to leave as soon as possible. Zechariah's nephew promised to take her and keep her safe. We made sure they had all they would need for the journey and I pressed some money into Mary's hand. "You never know what you might need," I whispered.

They left earlier today. I stepped outside to see them go. Mary turned and waved. Zechariah and I stood and watched until they rounded the olive trees near the well and disappeared. We stayed for a while, watching the birds as they circled and listening to the sounds of the village as it woke to a new day. Some children, screaming and laughing, ran past.

"Not long now," I said.

Joseph, the Husband of Mary

I KNEW MARY'S FAMILY well. Nazareth was much smaller in those days. She was the fiery one amongst her sisters; always quick to speak up if something wasn't right or someone wasn't being treated fairly. She had a few moments with some of the men when they thought they could push her around. We could all see her strength and her love of her people even when we were a community invaded and a people under Roman power.

No one expected her to fall in love with this carpenter; least of all, this carpenter. But love grew, and grew deep between us. Our families and friends, when they got over their surprise, celebrated our engagement with real joy.

That was the end of the expected things, the life we imagined together. Nothing was ever normal again for us.

I'll always remember the look on Mary's face when she told me of the angel and the voice; when she took my hand and held it to her belly and promised me that no man had given her the baby she knew she was carrying. There was fire in her eyes, but fear in her voice. She knew what this might mean. She knew I had the law on my side. She knew her life hung, entirely, in my hands.

I had to protect her. So, I planned a quiet ending to our engagement. I wondered about finding somewhere else to live and set up my workshop. Begin again. Far away. I didn't think I could bear to see her around. And I didn't want to watch her baby grow up.

But then I dreamed. The voice came in the darkness. God speaking. To me! It wasn't only Mary that God wanted! God wanted me as well! The two of us, together, making a family to welcome her baby, to keep him safe, to let him grow: "She'll bear a son. Name him Jesus, for he will save his people from their sins."

Many, many times, Mary and I would speak of how our life together began. We would remember our angels and our voices in the dark. We would wonder all over again at the risk God took with us. And we would remember, often, how the psalms we love summed up our story better than any of our own words could:

> "O sing to the Lord a new song; sing to the Lord, all the earth. Sing to the Lord, bless his name; tell of his salvation from day to day. Declare his glory among the nations, his marvelous works among all the peoples. For great is the Lord, and greatly to be praised; he is to be revered above all gods."[1]

Of all the people God could have chosen, of all the families God might have blessed, we were the ones! The Lord's greatness was never shown to me more powerfully than in his choosing of us. A nothing-special carpenter from nowhere important. A feisty young peasant woman having a baby out of wedlock. Me and Mary. It reminds me of all the times our people remember of God ignoring the mighty and working wonders through the lives of ordinary, humble folk. God loves to do the unexpected things, call the unlikely ones, bless those ignored by the world. Overturn everything.

But God's work was hard work for us too. Mary's pregnancy turned into endless traveling. There was her visit to Elizabeth and Zechariah when she was nearing her time. I didn't really want her to go, but it's hard to stop Mary when she's got a plan and gives you that look!

Then the Romans did as they often did; they reminded us who was in charge. This time it was a census and that meant registering where I came from. So, we packed up and walked the miles back to Bethlehem. I was working right up to the last moment, making beds for families expecting guests. We had no time to plan ahead.

Mary and I stumbled into Bethlehem late. I knew my family would already be overcrowded and we didn't want too many questions to face. We found a little inn. They didn't have a room, but they had animal pens and a little bit of shelter. And they had some kindness to spare.

That was where Jesus was born; amidst the hay and stink of animals, their breath like fog in the cold night air. Mary being brave but screaming. Me holding her, terrified. And then a beautiful baby boy, gulping air for the first time in his life. And his voice, his cries ringing into the dark. And the smell of him, and his head cradled in Mary's arms, his lips at her breast.

I don't know how much later it was when the shepherds came. We tried to get some sleep. But they tumbled out of the darkness, giggling and

---

1. Ps 96:1–4

staring and acting like they had just found treasure hidden in their fields. Eventually we got enough of their story to understand that God had told them our secret. And they now knew what we already knew. There would be times, in the years that followed, when Mary would watch Jesus playing or sleeping and, turning to me, would say again the words the angels taught those shepherds:

> "Do not be afraid; for see—I am bringing you good news of great joy for all the people: to you is born in the city of David a Savior, who is the Messiah, the Lord . . . Glory to God in the highest heaven, and on earth peace among those whom he favors."[2]

She never forgot those words. She needed them, sometimes, to hold on to when times got hard and Jesus was difficult to love. Or when her own fears and mine welled up and we needed to remember that he wasn't just our boy, he was God's Son. He had work to do beyond any carpentry I could teach him.

Later still, with a huge band of servants and followers, strangers came to us from the distant east. We couldn't understand most of what they said. They looked like no one we had ever seen before. And they left us with gifts; gifts fit for a king and gifts fit for a god and gifts fit for a funeral: gold, frankincense, and myrrh.

It was after they left that God turned my dreams into nightmares. Visions of soldiers. People screaming. Children dying. Herod knew about us, knew about Jesus. Herod always made his enemies disappear. So, one night, without telling a soul, we ran. We ran because our lives depended on it. We ran all the way to Egypt to make a sort of life with other refugees.

When news came that Herod was dead, Mary and I talked long and hard about what to do. Back we came. Make a home in Nazareth. Back to the workshop. Back to the familiar. Back to becoming just another family watching children playing.

Jesus is a young man now. He's a fine carpenter. He knows how to use the cedarwood, eucalyptus, and fir. He's learned to use the drawshave, ax, and saw. Mary fusses when he shakes the shavings and sawdust from his hair before a meal.

We're living with his secret. So far, we've kept it close and kept him safe. So far.

---

2. Luke 2:10b–14

A Girl Listening to John the Baptist

"Miriam! Miriam, come and see the wild man."

My brothers were the ones who called me and who took me down to the river that first time. I felt bad leaving Hannah to work with the others, but I wanted to see him because everyone was talking about him, and our family had been arguing about who he was. She just shrugged as I took my scarf and ran out into the courtyard.

It wasn't far from our home to the riverbank. Our farm is on the edge of Jericho and we can stand on the roof and see the river through the trees just a couple of miles away. As we walked together we joined a crowd, everyone babbling and laughing and enjoying something different. John was the man everyone was talking about; the desert man who appeared out of nowhere with his wild eyes and dirty hair and smell. He was something new, someone strange. He smashed up everything ordinary.

By the time we got to the Jordan the bank was filled with people. Some had climbed into the trees to get a better view. Others were sitting on the rocks or standing in whatever shade they could find. There were little children splashing and dancing and screaming in the shallows. Every now and then a pelican would swim past, eyes searching for fish, staying well away from the noise. It was a cloudy day, I remember, the sun as hot as always and the air sticky beside the water but the shadows coming and going as the clouds rolled in and out.

"There he is," Jacob pointed.

I had to shield my eyes. John was standing up to his knees in the river, surrounded by people. One by one, he and another man were leaning people down into the water until they went under completely. Then, just as quickly, they brought them back to their feet with the river making their hair flat and their clothes cling. Some were crying. Others smiled. John was talking softly to them all the time; we caught some words of prayer.

"What does it mean?"

"He does it for forgiveness," David said.

When the last person had been washed, John climbed out of the water and stood on a huge rock very close to where my brothers and I were watching. He started to speak then. His voice was strong and clear, with an accent I couldn't place. He told us that we were watching salvation come into the world. He said the things we were seeing and the words he was bringing were signs of God beginning something new and wonderful, scary too. He said that just as we all would wash the day's dirt away, just as we would prepare ourselves for prayer, so the washing that he brought was a baptism; a way to show we wanted to turn our lives around and be God's best friends.

"These people are your neighbors and your friends. Learn from them. See what they have done and do the same yourselves. Come to me with the bad things that you carry. Come to me with the shame that weighs you down. Come to me with the broken way your life has been. And you will find rest and peace and the forgiveness that changes everything. God is good but God is just. God sees and knows the things we hide and the shadows we are afraid to admit. Turn back to God then, all of you. Turn your life around. Offer yourself into the mercy and goodness of God, and God will welcome you and keep you safe. You will be forgiven, and all the bad and wrong in you will wash away like the dust in pure clear water."

The questions came then. Different people wanting to know more, trying to keep up with him.

Some asked what sort of life it was that his baptism began. "A life of generosity and truth," John said. He talked of giving to others, lending all we had to make someone else's life a little easier. He spoke of kindness. He told us how the world could be if we were looking out for each other the way God wanted us to.

As the questions kept coming, there were surprises. Some people asking the holy man about how to be good and how to be God's friends weren't the people I expected. "He attracts all kinds!" Jacob whispered. "It's like no one is too bad," I said. People muttered and looked cross when Matthew, one of the tax collectors, dared to speak up and asked if this baptism might even be for him. "Of course," said John. "But let it change the man you are. Show that you mean it. Never cheat anyone again." A soldier was standing there, his lance leaning against a tree. John told him never to use his power in the wrong way, never to frighten people or push people around or make them pay to be safe.

He got angry too. It wasn't all love and kindness. John came from the wilderness, and he didn't stay gentle and speak nicely all the time. His words could sting, like when you get told off for bad stuff. He spoke with power. It was like he was in a hurry and needed everyone to be in a hurry with him. The God John wanted us to give our lives to was a judging God, a God who saw it all and hated some of it. Turning around only makes sense if there are bad things to be sorry about. Forgiveness was big because there are big things wrong that need to be changed, big mistakes to be left behind. Even the Pharisees and Sadducees got it full blast when he saw them standing in the crowd. It's how we choose to live each day that God sees, not the people we are part of. What we do matters more than any name we have. Being part of God's people has to make us better day after day. That made us all quiet!

Someone suddenly asked him, "Are you the Messiah? Are you the one we've waited for?"

"The Messiah?" I asked my brothers. "Can he be?" "I don't know," David said.

John shook his head. "I'm here first because he's coming next. My work is making people ready to meet him. You come to me and to the river and the water tells a story of your lives made clean. But when he comes, the Messiah will do so much more. I'm a servant in the shade of his greatness. He will change you from the inside out. He'll give you the Spirit of Almighty God to change your lives for ever. He'll come as judge. He'll come as teacher. He'll come as healer. He'll come to save you from the bad, all of you. He'll see the heart of all things, see inside to what makes you who you are. He'll even see the stuff you want to hide. And he will know you, each one of you, and ask you to be his friends so he can be yours. He'll let you find out what God's love really means. My job is just to help you get started."

"When will this be?" a man called out.

"Soon. Very soon."

2

Christmas

The Innkeeper's Wife

THIS CENSUS IS GOOD business! We've never been so busy. Families coming from all over, hungry for space and for a good meal after eating dust. Plenty have a welcome ready in Bethlehem. They've people to stay with. For some, this count is a carnival. It's all about reunions and catching up with friends and neighbors and gossip. Fires burn long and we often hear singing. We've been picking up the people who can't get into the homes where their relatives already crowd.

Some arrivals aren't dancing. There are the bitter ones; this latest Roman edict another humiliation, another abomination forced by the empire and pandered to by our own leaders. For some, this travel is witness to just how lost and defeated our nation has become. We turned one of the really scary ones away. He was looking for trouble and we don't need trouble.

Then there are the lost ones. People who are just bewildered and afraid; worn out with miles and too much imagination. They've come back to a place they thought they need never see again. Bethlehem holds too many bad memories for them. We've a couple who ran away and now they're forced to be here all over again. I'm sorry for them. They look like something evil has been waiting here to greet them. They can't wait to run again.

Some have just got on with things, accepting all of this as but one more Roman nuisance. When so much of life is touched by the soldiers anyway, what's one more annoyance? Best to keep your head down, draw little attention and make the best you can. Survive!

So, we filled up pretty fast. Every space where folk could sleep taken. Food and drink meant constant trips to the market for our children to buy more. Sometimes our place seemed to be hovering on the edge of chaos. Voices got raised as tempers got short. My husband needing all of his patience and a bit of brawn. It is exhausting . . .

And then we got our baby.

It was late when his parents came to us. The streets had fallen quiet with just a few huddling down in corners to sleep where they could. Some soldiers loitered by the fire in the square beyond our door, playing dice and ignoring everyone. My husband opened up when they kept knocking. They had traveled from Nazareth. He was familiar. Joseph, the carpenter's son. I didn't know her. But the weight and the worry of the baby inside her had her huddling by his side. Exhaustion bent her. My husband took pity. Hard not to, even though we were full. He sent them to the animal pens to find whatever warmth and shelter they could. And a little bit of privacy.

As the night deepened, I kept an eye on her. I took round some blankets, a bit of food, water. This was her first. They were clinging to each other and waiting in the dark. Fear was with them both. It got to me too. It was when I was bringing a fresh lamp that her time came. I could hear her before I rounded the corner. She was kneeling in the straw and mud, wet and frightened. Joseph was behind her, his arms under her shoulders, trying to speak words of calm without knowing what to say. They were so small against the night, bound together, vulnerable and uncertain.

I knew I wasn't leaving until this finished, one way or the other. Babies are born all the time in all sorts of places. Death visits plenty of families; baby or mother or both. I remembered my three times. I remembered some of what the midwives said and how they worked with me. I remembered the excruciating pain and the ecstasy and the exhaustion. I felt the fear that she was feeling as a mirror of my own.

I ran back to warn my husband and returned with fresh water and clean blankets. I knelt in front of her, promising that all would be well. Empty words, bundled in my hope and worry. In the flickering light, with the animals breathing into the air around us, I wiped her face, stroked her hair, held her crushing hand as she screamed and panted.

"Breathe, Mary."

"You're doing well, so well."

"Not long now."

"Push."

"Keep pushing, that's it."

"So close now."

"Come on Mary, not much longer."

Then the waiting. Mary crying and Joseph kissing her cheek and shushing with the softness of a lover. We would wriggle as we tried to get as comfortable as the cold night and the straw and the stone let us. My husband hovered, wanting to help but wanting to be anywhere else. I remember looking at the stars so bright.

Another spell of struggling and pushing, panting and screaming. Time escaping into the pain and the night.

And then I was holding a slimy head in my trembling fingers, wiping dark hair, staring at a face never seen before. Eyes tight shut. I ran my finger into the tiny mouth, cleaning out the mess, praying for a breath. A rush of limbs and body and there he was. A boy! A baby boy covered in blood and slime, kicking in my arms. Mary lay back into Joseph. They were both staring and crying. Laughing too. I gently lifted him up and into Mary's waiting arms. She bent over him feeling the warmth and wetness of his life, smelling him. And he mewed and wriggled and we knew that the miracle had happened.

I cut him from her and wrapped them in a blanket. As he squirmed and sucked in his first mouthfuls of cold night air, he howled. Mary and Joseph wrapped him close, leaning together, lost in wonder and relief.

I stayed a while, cleaning up and doing what I could to make them comfortable. My husband put his arm around me, whispered, "Well done."

We slipped away, leaving them to each other with our goats for company. Mary's voice caught me in the dark: "Thank you."

A Shepherd from Bethlehem

EVERYONE SEEMS TO REMEMBER our rejoicing. We woke up many as we ran the streets and shouted the news. Plenty of curses followed us, but that wasn't so unusual. When you spend so much time out with the flocks and herds, away from the warmth and routines of homes, wrapped in the stench, you don't always fit with everything acceptable and proper. What few people know about is our fear.

Bethlehem was noisy and choked as the census drew so many back. We watched as they straggled over the hills for days. There were the lonely walkers and the chattering families. Some camped and lit their fires up in the hills with us. Others hurried on, eager to get indoors ahead of the night and looking for the warmth of family and friends.

That particular night was really cold. We built up the fire and wrapped our cloaks close to keep the chill away. You could see the breath rising from the animals as they huddled down in their groups. We could see the houses below, a few specks of light in the dark as some left lamps in their windows for a welcome. Above us the stars made a roof for the world, impossibly clear. Our conversation slowed and stuttered. The silence of the hills settled over everything.

I was dozing when the light began.

You know that way in which you can tell it is getting lighter even with your eyes shut? That was it. As I came to, I was assuming I must have drifted off and now the dawn was breaking. But it wasn't the dawn. No sun was rising. All of us were on our feet then, staring, terrified. The animals sensed and saw it too, we could hear their restlessness and fear.

The light was growing all around us. It was shifting all the time, like a river in the sky. I tried to see where it was coming from. If this was a storm it was a storm unlike any we had ever known, and we had been in plenty of them. There was no sudden flash of lightning. There was no thunder. If anything, the silence was the worst of it. How can the world burn without a sound?

The sky was now washed in rippling layers of light. The stars were still there, but we were seeing them shining behind curtains of light. We turned around and saw that the curtains were hanging right around us. The whole hillside was touched by them. From high in the sky they dropped down to flow over the stones and dust and grass. The light broke around the branches of the old oaks, shining off the leaves like they were beaten metal in the brightest sun.

Worse came then.

We were no longer on our own. As the hillside blazed around us, we could see figures moving. They were walking in a wide circle. We couldn't see their faces. "Romans?" whispered David. Maybe that was it. Some legion was on the march and somehow lit the night to see their way. "Maybe," I whispered back. But there was no sound of footfall, no clink of metal on the stones, no noise of packs and shields and leather and swearing. Just the silence, impossibly deep.

One figure stepped closer, and we shrank back. My hand went to my dagger and others raised their sticks. Someone grabbed a burning branch from the fire and held it out, the flames rustling and dancing. It was strange, but the coming attack was welcome because at least we knew what it meant to defend our flocks. The wild and the thieving had taught us. We were ready.

But the voice! It came from this stranger we could barely see as the light danced and we struggled to take things in. Not a Roman soldier's mockery. Not the gang leader's opening bargain. A different sort of voice. A command and an invitation, a kind of song, a priest's blessing and a child's laughter: "Do not be afraid!"

What a word! And yet, somehow, the fear was slipping away. "I am bringing you good news of great joy for all the people." Hands and shoulders relaxed. The burning branch was tossed back into the fire where it flared up and sent sparks leaping. I let go of my dagger. What was this? "To you is born this day in the city of David a Savior, who is the Messiah, the Lord."

We were staring and wondering and overwhelmed.

"This will be a sign for you: you will find a child wrapped in bands of cloth and lying in a manger."[1]

---

1. Luke 2:12

Such madness! None of this made any sense at all. We all knew about the Messiah of course. How can you grow up around here and not have the dreams told and told until they become part of you? We knew the hopes that one would come to set us free. We knew that we were meant to be a people of patience, a waiting nation. One day, he would come. All this we knew. But on a hillside outside Bethlehem with a bunch of shepherds and an army made of starlight? And a baby sleeping where the cattle eat?

Even as the thoughts were swirling, they had started singing. They sang in words we could not understand. Sometimes it was as soft and sweet as the lonely bird high in the sky. Sometimes it roared like the might of the storm clouds. It rose and fell around us. And, sometimes, we understood. "Glory to God in the highest heaven, and on earth peace among those whom he favors."[2]

It went on and on. Singing and movement and light and something beautiful. It wrapped around the hillside and settled deep inside each one of us. It was agony when the silence swallowed their music and they stepped away. The light began to fade until all that was left was us beneath the stars and the change within. We were in a hurry then. We drew lots to see who had to stay to guard the flocks. Then we were running for the silent houses down below.

We all knew where to go. We had heard their story when a few of us had gone to the market. Behind the old inn a couple had camped. She was expecting. It was the obvious place. We found them there; saw him. We told them what had happened. They listened hard. And then we were running again, dancing, shouting. We banged the doors. We laughed. We shouted: "He's here!" We tried to wake Bethlehem with our joy.

2. Luke 2:14

Anna Greets the Baby Jesus in the Temple

I HAVE LEARNED TO live into my name. To be the one called "favor" when you have lived as long as I have as a widow takes a lot of learning. The seven years of our marriage were joy to us both. The many more years since have tested me beyond belief. And yet, woven into the heartache, has come a thread of blessing and a calling that has sustained me.

My course was different to so many others. At first, as is the way, I tried to settle with family and friends. My son took me into his home and the neighbors were kind. My father's people did all they could. Phanuel was so worried about me. I know I didn't ease his mind with my own restlessness. How I wish he had known a little of the peace I discovered before the Lord took him. I will always regret some of the things I said to him when the anger at my loss burned in me like a fire in the depths of night.

But I could not settle. Would not settle. I felt that there was something different for me than watching the children of others growing up and making myself as useful as I might be. It was the story of Samuel and Hannah that kept coming to me. I thought of her consecrating her son to the Lord at his house in Shiloh and of him growing up there, surrounded by the prayers and offerings of the people, learning the ways of worship from old Eli. I thought of Hannah finding it within herself to let go of so much in thanksgiving for what the Lord had done. I thought of life as being lent from the Lord for a time; not ours to hoard and possess and dominate, but ours to discover and offer. And a longing began in me.

I remember when the prophecies first came. It was whilst my mourning was still young. A few had gathered and I was listening as they argued about the scroll we had heard in the synagogue that Sabbath. Then, so suddenly that it shocked us all, I was talking. I was proclaiming that the Lord did notice us in our suffering and loss. It was a word of faith that seemed to linger in the air in the silence that followed. That was where it began. Other times followed; more words of witness. People started to visit the house, ask for me, ask me for advice. I gained a reputation, even a little fame and following.

The more I heard the word "prophet" attached to my name, the more my longing for time and space with the Lord grew. The more people came to seek me out, the more I thought of Hannah giving up her son Samuel, the more I dreamed of him living in the sanctuary and devoting himself to prayer and service. The quiet beauty of our village overlooking the sea seemed increasingly to feel no longer home to me. I was out of place.

The family, I think, were not surprised when I told them of my decision. The Temple authorities had heard of my witness and welcomed me warmly when we reached Jerusalem. They had made a room ready for me, close to the portico. And that is how my life began this new chapter.

A rhythm slowly established itself for me. Devoting yourself to the Lord is demanding work. It has its high and holy days when the world is awash with glory and the prayers seem to cascade like a never-ending waterfall of sweetest adoration. But it has plenty of other days when the cold of the night has made sleep impossible and the dawn brings resentments and the mind wanders amidst the worship and those around are infuriating in so many ways. There were times, plenty, when I wondered if I had got things wrong. Could the Lord truly want this of me? Was my life one of devotion or one of arrogant self-serving? Was I really the humble servant of the Lord that folk spoke of or was I delighting in my own reputation for holiness? There were days which grew into weeks when no word came.

But perhaps it is even more in these empty times that faith can find its footholds. When there is nothing to confirm the risk we have taken in trusting, then it is that trusting is all we have. So, I trusted. And I went on. And the days became months, and the months became years. And I settled. And it grew to be good as my faith fell deeper and my heart grew more open to the things the Lord was showing me.

I believe all of this was preparing me for yesterday.

She was a young village mother, shy and nervous in the Temple. Close beside her was her husband. Mary and Joseph had come to do as ritual required and make their sacrifices. I was watching them across the courtyard when they were presented to Simeon. Something in his reaction rooted me to the spot. He took their baby in his old hands and bowed his head. I could not hear what he was saying, but I saw what it did to his parents.

Running, I joined them as they made their little huddle in the afternoon sunshine. Doves were circling in the bluest of skies. Simeon, the tears wetting his cheeks, turned to greet me. In his arms lay a baby boy. "He has come at last," Simeon said.

As he handed the child back to Mary, I reached out and touched my finger to the tiny forehead, felt a wisp of hair. His eyes were open, staring, unafraid. Mary was looking at me, the questions hovering between us.

"I have prayed in this place for this day for a long time," I said to her. "Before you were born, I came here to dedicate the rest of my life to our Lord. I have waited and I have prayed. I have hoped and I have prayed. The prophecies of my sisters and brothers have told us what we wait for: a savior and a redeemer. The time will come, we have been taught, when the Lord will save us just as our people were saved from their slavery in Egypt. Just as Miriam sang when our people were set free, so I have been singing the songs of the Lord in the hope that I might live to see our freedom come. And, today, it has come."

By now, Mary was hugging the baby close, and Joseph had his arm around them both. Simeon was nodding, his face a picture!

"What do you name him?" I asked.

"Jesus," Mary whispered.

"The Lord saves," I echoed. "It is the perfect name."

"It was not ours to give," Joseph added. "It was what we were told to call him."

"Our names can say so much about who we are, and who we will become," I replied.

Simeon and I watched them leave. We stood for a long time together as the Temple grew quieter around us. Another day in the house of the Lord was drawing to its close. But, for five of us at least, the dawn was just breaking.

Mary, the Mother of Jesus, in Egypt

FRANKINCENSE, MYRRH, AND GOLD would take some explaining here!

A little family on the run, parents with a toddler, can go unnoticed. We have learned how to make ourselves as invisible as possible. We have fitted in to our new home. But if ever anyone discovered what we hide in the sack beneath the floor, then we would be in trouble.

To my surprise, it really has become home to us. Our people in Mendes have welcomed us. They are used to Jews arriving from the east. Enough news has come of the growing madness of Herod and the cruelty of Rome to stifle questions when a new family appear, exhausted from the long road, desperate for shelter. We share the silence and make a life. We join the times of prayer. We speak of the dreams of Jerusalem but know that we will not be joining any pilgrimage. How strange, to make a home in the very place that once our people fled; to flee from the promised land seeking sanctuary back where we were slaves.

Egypt is a wealthy province and, as long as the harvests are good, as long as the Nile's banks are green, the Romans seem satisfied and quiet. The grain stores are busy and the boats ply their trade. Mendes must hold so many secrets with all of the caravans and merchants passing through. Joseph chose wisely. Of course he did! This is a place big enough for a child to vanish, big enough for a family to become unremarkable. And it is a place where a good carpenter, reliable and skilled, can arrive with nothing and find work.

My Joseph has done so much to keep us safe! And now, we rejoice as a new baby grows in me, a brother or sister for Jesus. God is good! I am glad for us all, but especially that Joseph will be a father now. He does so well with Jesus, but I know that it is hard for him.

I watch Jesus as he sleeps, the lamp light flickering on his face as he sucks his thumb the way he often does. He will have no memories of how his life began and how close he came to death. We will not scare him with the story.

It was another night in Bethlehem. We were settled there with Joseph's family. It was never easy because the baby's birth had left so many things unspoken and so many things unexplained. The shepherds had seen to that! But Joseph's family are good people, and they welcomed his skills and his hard work. All that changed when the strangers rode in. Their caravan stretched off into the darkness. Soldiers and servants, camels and donkeys, gold and jewels glittering. They were strange in every way. We could not understand them unless the servant from the palace translated for us. Even then, we only caught a little of their story. They scared me with their magic and their talk of stars. They knew things that frightened us.

We were keeping the truth about Jesus such a close secret, buried in our hearts. Yet they were on their knees in front of him. They did not share our faith or even know the God whose people we are. Yet here they were, so far from home, worshipping the child our God had made in me. There were gasps from our family when the gifts came out; gifts fit for a king. I doubt that any home in Bethlehem had such wealth as we had then. It made all of us uneasy. Riches are harder to hide than people.

I wasn't surprised when Joseph told me of his dream. Another angel. Another message. Another dose of chaos! We hurried our goodbyes and felt the relief from those who waved us off. We all knew the danger we had become. We prayed for safety as much for those staying in Bethlehem as for us upon the road. We hoped we might take trouble away with us. Our escape might let the story get forgotten. We asked God to protect us all.

Sunrise saw us already on the way. We made slow progress. The donkey was old and we were carrying all we could because we knew we had to make a home with what we had. We tried to avoid too many encounters as we made our way slowly along the roads that led to the coast. When it was too hot, we turned aside and Joseph would rig a cover for us all. Jesus was starting to walk by then. He would pull himself up and bump around on the rug. His head was often too heavy and he would tumble backwards with a look of complete surprise. Sometimes, his falls would end in tears and howls, sometimes with giggling. I would often hold him as I fed the donkey, and he would reach his hand out and she would nuzzle.

But the road is a hard place, and we had nothing against the storms when they came. The small fire we risked did little to keep the cold away at night. We bundled Jesus in blankets and shivered on the ground. We met more than one who would have robbed us if it were not for Joseph and the knife he showed. Roman soldiers passed us. But we always moved aside, and they barely glanced our way. We were just another peasant family on the move.

Turning west, we joined the road along the coast. I had never seen the ocean. Nor had Joseph. It dazzled us by day and lulled us to sleep in the night. It made me feel very small, and very far from Nazareth.

Things became more difficult when we finally approached the mighty fortresses of Pelusium. There were more questions here than we had faced since leaving Bethlehem. We were terrified that, somehow, Herod would have spies waiting for a family protecting a baby boy. So, we told the usual lies. We had come from Ekron, forced to move to seek work. We had made our way westwards and had family in Egypt. They were waiting for us. It was plausible enough.

And now, here we are, as safe as anywhere and safer than back home. Joseph mends what needs mending and makes what folk require. I have made friends and we share in watching our children as they play. There is food on our table and a roof to keep us warm. The fire stays lit and the lamps are welcoming. Jesus plays and grows and has his tantrums and hums his tunes and smiles. And my belly grows with his playmate.

It might be good here. But here can never, truly, be our home. And Joseph told me this morning of his dream. That man and his dreams! But they have been trustworthy every time. If it is true that Herod is dead, the way back opens for us. By the time we get there, Jesus will be nearly three and his brother or sister will help us blend in. We will be the couple who went away for the census and came back a family! People will wonder where we've been. We'll need a new story that sounds convincing.

And, under the rug in a hole we'll carefully dig in the floor, we'll hide a sack of treasure fit for a king.

3

Epiphany

One of the Magi

I HAVE SPENT so long working with these archives that they have become my world. Sometimes, after my studies with the manuscripts have held me captive through days and nights, I emerge into the light and find myself a stranger to my own time. The ancient texts tell of wonders and heroics, tragedies and disasters, gods and omens, spirits and magic. They people our past with names long forgotten and realms long dissolved. They speak of who we are and how we got to be who we are. And, if you have the skills and the patience, they open windows into the future.

But it is very strange to find myself adding to the store of knowledge in this way. We agreed, as our caravan finally split up and we each settled to our journeys home, that we would record all that had come to pass over the incredible months of our odyssey. Soon, these words of mine will be sealed into the pots and placed in the vault. I have been a traveler across these stories. I never thought to write my own.

When it first revealed itself, the star was so low on the western horizon that it was easily missed. The sharp eyes of the apprentices spotted it first. Something new in the heavens! Certainly a portent. But was this messenger sent as invitation or warning? We pored over the star maps. We dove deep into the records to see if such a thing had come before. We measured and recorded. We watched as it rose slowly higher and grew slowly brighter.

Others were watching and wondering. Word came from other cities and other palaces as travelers passed through. Theories and predictions flourished in those early months. Prophecies were called upon as fuel for argument. The spell casters worked with their potions and entrails and fell into their trances. The military worried about unrest and invasion. Farmers feared for harvests.

The brighter the star, the more it came to dominate so much. Eventually my master gathered some of us in the clear night of the palace gardens and asked what we should do. Others had come from many places to share their wisdom and offer a little of their fear. Very quickly we agreed that answers would be found where the star was leading. But, where was that?

A scroll was placed upon the table. The old man had been a trusted adviser for as long as any of us could remember. A Jew, he had been bought as a boy from slavers as they headed east. The years and his character had blessed him. His god protected him, and his wits outdistanced many. He had become as trusted as any who served my master. Now, with a power that trembled in his voice and tears on his cheeks, he begged to read from the words of his own people. So it was, with the star above and the fragrance of the frangipani on the breeze, with the fountains playing and the lamps glowing, that I heard the prophecy that would start the journey that changed my life.

Eli read: "The scepter shall not depart from Judah, nor the ruler's staff from between his feet, until tribute comes to him; and the obedience of the peoples is his."[1] Could it be? A king to rule the Jews and more than the Jews? The sky proclaiming his birth?

By the time the light of dawn was showing it was agreed. A party would be sent to seek the truth. We would gather several who had studied these things and create a caravan with servants and soldiers to head toward the west. We would take with us gifts fit for a king. Some were still doubtful, but many of us believed that Eli pointed to a truth worth testing. I was one chosen to go.

In the end, we would be away from our homes for more than half a year. It was the farthest most of us had ever been, although some of the servants had worked the trade routes even farther. Some had knowledge of the places we were passing through. Most of the time, we could make ourselves understood in the communities we met. Food and water were our greatest treasures; guarded and rationed. We would try to find shade when the sun was highest. At night we would mark the star and check our progress against its course. The days flowed into an endless walking and riding like a river without beginning and without end. Camp was set and the fires were lit. The fires were covered, the tents were packed and on again. On and on . . .

We faced the storms when the sand became blinding and found its way into every fold and crease. Valleys of bare rock with no sign of life became torrents of water as rivers newly born echoed with distant rains.

1. Genesis 49:10

Bandits tried, several times, to plunder our supplies, steal our animals, and cut our throats. We were glad that the soldiers remained vigilant even as I was appalled by their cruelty. Sometimes it was the Roman forts along the road that came to our aid. We always kept our quest to ourselves, speaking of the markets we hoped to supply if fortune and the gods looked sweetly.

So it was that we came into the lands of the Jews. We made our way to Jerusalem, the walls gleaming as the afternoon sun began to paint them in peach and pink. We had prepared for what we knew would be our most vital conversation. The old king received us with a welcome that hid little of his dreadful hunger. Herod's reputation traveled well ahead of him. We knew his love of violence, and his declining health in body and in mind made him even more unpredictable and dangerous. Several times in the days we spent at court we were awakened by screams from his dungeons chilling the night.

We did not want to bring him news of a rival. But we needed the wisdom locked within the archives of his palaces and temples. We did not know enough to find our final miles. Eventually, we got the name we needed. He gave us a guide to take us there. He charged us to bring him confirmation. He watched us go.

Bethlehem is not a big place. They say its name means "House of Bread." More questioning finally brought us to a home. With the moon full and the new star outshining every other star in the heavens, we left our party making camp and lighting fires. We walked across the dust and dung to where lamps flickered in the window. A man opened the door.

What we found were new peasant parents and their baby boy, their firstborn. They were called Joseph and Mary. The baby they named Jesus. We were unsurprised when the name was explained to us, "the deliverer." Somehow, it was fitting that this child whose birth lit the heavens and unsettled kingdoms should be discovered cradled in the arms of a village girl sleeping in a nowhere place. None of us doubted that this was where we were meant to be. This was our destination; he was our destination. We were as far from palaces and power as it was possible to be. We were nowhere special. And yet . . .

And yet here we were, crammed into this tiny house, kneeling before this baby, whispering, gazing in wonder. We, who knew so much, we who gave counsel to kings and queens, we who guarded our secrets and guided nations in our worship of the gods, captured and entranced by a foreigner baby.

Finally, we opened up the saddle bags and brought out the gifts we had been carrying all those miles: gold, frankincense, myrrh. Tokens of welcome. Gifts for a king. Offerings for a god. Wide-eyed, his parents listened silently as Herod's guide translated our story and our wonderment. And Jesus? He woke and cried and nursed at her breast and ignored us completely.

The next day found us already on the road before sunrise, heading home. We were taking care to disappear. Dreams in the night had woken one of us. Herod's jealousy had to be deflected. The captain of our guard made sure that Herod's guide would never tell anyone anything.

Now, here I am, writing it down so that others might read it one day.

And I am left to wonder at all that might be.

King Herod the Great

I AM SATISFIED NOW.

The report is clear. Bethlehem has been cleansed. This threat, at least, is over. There will always be others. I am surrounded by traitors and plotters. I know that. I know many would delight to see the sword at my throat. Even my own family have tried. And failed. I need to have the eyes and ears of the palace always open, always attentive. Whispers; listen to the whispers! Others have plotted and schemed and sought after outsiders to do their dirty work. Spies and informants earn their keep and Eliel keeps the guards on their toes. I know where to find loyalty and I reward it. And I know how to deal with treachery. You can't build a great house without great sacrifice. God is my witness; my kingdom shall prosper. My time may be ending, my powers failing more than many have seen, but still I shape destiny. And my name will not die.

Two years is a long time to let a rebellion fester. Maybe he wasn't really that old, but why take the risk? Better to wipe out a few dozen boys and make sure rather than have him loitering in some filthy shadow, learning the arts and sharpening his blade. No harm in having the story of Bethlehem become a warning people tell. No harm in having everyone remember. A restless people need plenty of stories to help them remember why obedience matters. Some of the men probably went too far, but even that is useful. Love is easy to find and just as easy to lose. Fear makes for something stronger, more enduring, harder to undermine. I can build with their fear. Just as Rome does.

That was quite a morning when their caravan approached the city. The first reports had come in days before. We didn't know who they were, but they didn't seem heavily armed and so we let them trail their way from place to place. Unusually for traders, they didn't seem to know where the best markets were. That got them noticed. Slowly, they became more and

35

more strange, more of a threat. They weren't trying to sell much at all. In fact, most of the time, they simply bought food and had their animals tended to. So, we watched, and we waited, and we listened.

Just as well.

They gave themselves away. Translating for them as they stopped at yet another synagogue, my man finally heard the heart of what they planned. "King of the Jews!" Some foreign power sending fools to find a way to start a revolution. Some baby pretender hidden until the day he was big enough and strong enough to raise his army. Some puppet waiting for his master. They looked and sounded harmless enough with their silks and gems, their talk of stars and wonders. They cast themselves as mystics and wizards but I could see through every curtain of their flimsy magic. We needed to know more. So, the plan was obvious. Draw them in. Bring them to Jerusalem. Pamper and flatter and be patient. Convince them they had happened upon friends. Let them betray themselves.

It worked, almost.

A royal escort met them on the Mount of Olives and their train became a state procession. Pennants flying, marching to the drumbeats, a crowd quickly arranged. I watched them from the balcony and met them in the Hall of Cedars. Solomon would have been proud! We shone with the gold of the palace and the wealth of the welcome. I made it as clear as I could through the translators that they were guests honored here for as long as they wished. We gave them a couple of days and then held the first great banquet to receive them. The more they settled in, the more they wanted to talk. Easy!

Five of them seemed to be the leaders. They had come from the far east, they claimed. Certainly, their tongues and dress were exotic. Stargazers and wise men, they told their tale of watching a new light burn in the sky and they took it for a sign. Something compelled them to follow it. I never really heard them explain why. Of course, they couldn't. They were trying to avoid catching themselves out in their own lies. We had seen their star. Now they were turning it into doom.

"Where is the child who has been born king of the Jews?" That was our way in. I called the council and the priests together. We sent the scribes off to scour their books. My fears grew. The whispers around me started. Several times, the wisest started to talk about the promise of the Messiah. They fell silent just as quickly, but the point was made. Terror was brooding over me, seeping from the shadows.

Messiah! More than a king. More than a rival. Greater than anyone I have ever had to fight. If the people dared to let him be, this one could become a destroyer in the hands of God. One to rally every heart that longed for something more than my affection or my payment or my fury. One who came to overthrow. One who rode the fires of the sky and who commanded the flood. The leader of angels. I didn't need the scribes and priests to paint the picture. I knew enough of their prophecies. I have used them often enough. All these years I have worked my own magic, kept Rome where I wanted and the people where I needed. I know how to make things come true. Hoping for a Messiah is dangerously potent magic, poison in the soul of a nation.

No sleep. Long watches on the palace ramparts staring at that cursed light blazing in mockery over me. Traitors circling. God taunting. I knew the abyss awaiting me in this threat. Even the rumor of him could be enough.

Simple then. Kill the rumor.

The next day the scribes returned with what we needed: Bethlehem! Hidden away in the scrolls of Micah, they said.

That night I called the five of them once more, pretending secrecy. I held myself well enough to fool them one last time. I stressed the importance and the need for haste. Ancient prophecy was coming true, and we needed to take care not to derail the will of God. I told them how wonderful their mission had become for me and all my people. I spoke of ancient dreams fulfilled, generations of longing finding their time. They needed to go and discover the boy and bring me news so that I could go and worship him. Their wonderment and homage must pave the way for mine and for all our people. We sent them on their way that night with no great noise. But Eliel ensured their new guide was one of our best.

We waited. One day became two, then four. Too long! We sent others to find them. They reported nothing. The strangers had made it to Bethlehem, but then they had vanished as if they had never been at all. Of our spy there was neither sign nor news. He had either been discovered and killed or had betrayed me. My fury knew no limits.

Everyone in the palace will remember those days.

Everyone in Bethlehem will never forget.

James, Looking Back Upon the Transfiguration

JESUS WOULD OFTEN TAKE the three of us aside, let us be particularly close. That made us arrogant sometimes. I know. We felt ourselves to be his special ones; the very trusted three. He would slap us down for it. We deserved that. But there were things the three of us got to know and got to see that no one else was there for. We're all his witnesses now, as you know. But the three of us have a little more to share, something of the inside of things, the stuff the world and our friends can only ever hear about. We were there. And he wanted us to be. He wanted some things to be private when they happened. But he wanted us to be there with him so that we could tell the story when the time came.

We were the ones he took into the room when he took the hand of little dead Elizabeth and told her to get up. We were the ones who stood there stunned as Jairus and Miriam fell to their knees and smothered her in gratitude and disbelief. It was just the three of us that final night who joined him in the heart of Gethsemane so that we might watch his prayers of life and death. Which made the three of us especially guilty of failing him, of course.

And there was that other time.

We had been wandering around the villages of Caesarea Philippi. By then, Jesus was well known, and we gained a crowd pretty much wherever we went. People would come to listen to him teach. Some would dive in to debate and question and argue with him. He loved those times! They would bring the sick and the possessed. And some would be unconvinced and hostile. We had got used to the mix. Jesus took us all aside for one of the quieter times; just us and him and the peace of the field. I remember that he asked us what people were saying about him, who they thought he was. We broke the rumors and the gossip to him: one of the greats brought back to life; John the Baptist maybe; Elijah; another of the prophets. He laughed. And us? Who did we think he was? Peter said it but we were all thinking it: "Messiah!" No sooner said, then he was off on what became the regular warning we always refused to heed. He was the suffering Savior; the Messiah who would die and rise again. So obvious now. So impossible then.

A week or so passed. We were in the Jezreel Valley, walking amidst the fields and groves of olives. It was early in the afternoon, the sun high and the day truly hot. It seemed a perfect moment to find a cool bit of shade and doze off. We were even dumping our packs and getting settled when Jesus called the three of us. "Come with me," he said. Assuming he wanted a quiet word, we followed as he wandered away.

Except he wasn't wandering at all. Instead, he straightened up and started marching us toward the hill that dominates that part of the land. We started asking questions and he just kept saying that there were things we needed to know. Lessons are fine. We were learning all the time. But what was so useful about climbing an exhausting path when the others were relaxing? This was special treatment the three of us didn't warm to in the heat of the day!

The climb took us up a goat track as it straggled toward the top. We had to go in single file and I was at the back. Every now and then we stopped to catch our breath and take in the view. It was quite a view to take in. Off in the distance, vague in the haze but still visible, was Nazareth. We seemed to be the only people on the move. We imagined we could see our friends as they slept right where we wanted to be. And then the path leveled off and we were on the top; a great flat expanse of trees and scrub and rock and a mosaic of flowers dancing in the gentle breeze. It felt good to let the wind cool us and we turned our faces into it for sheer relief.

Jesus walked on a little. The three of us ambled behind, wondering what this was all about. Where did he want to get to? It wasn't so much about getting somewhere. It was more that he needed to be in the right place to receive something. He stopped and spread his arms wide and turned to face us. "Your face!" John mumbled. All three of us just stared. That familiar face was hard to look at. All of him was hard to look at. There was a searing brightness, as if the sun had fallen and consumed where he had been. No heat, just the dazzling light. We staggered away, tripping over each other as we did.

Peter was the one to see that we were not alone any more. Two others had silently walked into the glare and were talking with Jesus. Peter has always said, ever since, that he has no idea why he thought they were Moses and Elijah. Maybe he was remembering how Jesus would sometimes teach us of how he was leading a new exodus like Moses had done; setting everyone free from sin and shame, a new Moses guiding slaves out of today's captivity. And Jesus was so aware of all of the prophets and their messages of hope and judgment. Why not imagine that this must be the greatest prophet of them all? And hadn't we just been saying, only a few days before, that people thought Jesus might be Elijah come again?

Peter tried to cling to something tangible amidst this mystery by offering to make shelters there and then. John and I didn't think it a particularly useful response, but we weren't arguing! Even as the words were fresh, the sky began to close around our hilltop. Clouds rolled in, a cloth of glowing gold and yellow that seemed to settle all around. And in the cloud, amidst the light where everything was hard to see, we heard a voice as clear as if the speaker was standing at our side:

"This is my Son, the Beloved; listen to him!"[1]

That had us cowering. We had spent long enough with Jesus to know that he made heaven and earth touch and mingle in ways that defied explanation. He worked wonders and carried God's blessing and authority everywhere in the ways we carried our possessions. He was the one through whom the power and presence of God could reach into all the lives he met and all the homes he visited. His touch was the touch of healing and his words spoke with the authority of Scripture. He made God's words become reality. He brought the majesty of holiness into every morning and into every home.

But this was so much more than we had met before; more than we had ever seen in him. This was affirmation and confirmation of everything we thought to be true. It was as if God was listening when we had called him the Messiah, and now God wanted us to see and feel all that name conjured. He was the one in whom all that is of God and all that is of earth get held together. He was God and he was humanity all at the same time. And, on that hilltop, the mask was lifted and we saw and heard the truth.

Everything stopped as suddenly as it began. It was just the four of us late in the afternoon of that same day. Silent now, Jesus led us down again. About halfway he stopped and we all stared out across the plain. This time

1. Mark 9:7b

we could definitely see the others sitting together beside the olives. "Keep this to yourselves," he commanded. And that is what we did. The three of us held this secret just like the other secrets he shared with us. We waited, as he told us to, until all his glory was revealed. We waited for his cross. We waited for his resurrection. We kept this to ourselves. And then we started to talk about it, bearing witness to the wonder of it all.

Jesus loved to play with words. He was a master with them. And he enjoyed playing games with them too. Pretty early on, he gave my brother and I one of his nicknames. So, we became the sons of Boanerges, the sons of Thunder. We could be argumentative. We could be loud, and we could be rash. We were arrogant, and we've plenty to regret. But on that secret hilltop, just for a moment, Jesus let us see the truth. He let us see all that he was, and all that he is. He let us see through this world into all that lies beyond. He entrusted us with himself. And that's what we've been sharing ever since. Let the truth ring out!

4

Lent

The Samaritan Woman at the Well

SYCHAR IS NEVER GOING to be the same again. Few of us are ever going to be the same again. Something has begun in me, something amazing, something pure and good and beautiful. Something I never expected. A pure gift.

It started three days ago, about noon. As usual, I went on my own to fetch the day's water from Jacob's well. I try to avoid the busy times when the others come in the cool of the morning and evening. I don't like being around when everyone else gathers to chat and gossip with their children playing. I've endured too many looks, overheard too many whispers. Everyone thinks they know all about me, and what they think they know makes me dirty and them suspicious. In this life, how others see us can make us into things we don't want to be.

I saw him from a long way off. A man, sitting on the side of the well, his head covered against the sun. That made me nervous. He was watching me as I approached. That made me even more nervous. From his clothes I could see he was a Jew, and I guessed he was a rabbi.

Jewish rabbi. Man. Alone. Me, a Samaritan, and a woman, and alone. He was in the wrong place. I assumed he would get up and leave. The last thing he would want was anything to do with me. And I didn't particularly want anything to do with him. But he was in the business of demolishing everything I feared and everything I thought about myself and about Jews and about God. He came along to undo the stuff that was wrong.

He kept it simple to begin with. "Give me a drink," he asked with a smile and a hand reaching toward the jar I was carrying. I stared. I hugged the jar close as if to protect myself from him. Was this a trick?

I don't mind standing up for myself. I've had to, often, and often with men. I've felt the sting of Jewish rejection of Samaritans. And I've dished out my share of our rejection of Jews. So, I told him, stop playing games.

But he didn't stop. Already he was unpicking things by the well of Jacob. He was giving me time, showing respect. I had his complete and utter attention. It felt as if, in the heat of the day in the wrong place, I was the whole reason he was here. He was looking right at me, as if this conversation was anything but an accident. And what he seemed to see made him want to talk with me.

By now we were talking about different kinds of water. He said he had some of his own, hinting that he could be the one to give me a drink. I pointed out that he didn't even have a bucket! I challenged him then. If he wanted to work wonders, let him prove he was greater than Jacob himself. Looking back now, I see what was happening. He was starting with everything I knew and inviting me further. His "living water" had me wondering.

And, only then, only after we had danced with each other for a while, only after I had begun to really listen, only then did he reveal himself. He let us weave the trust together, let me share with him, relishing our competition. He wasn't trying to win an argument or score his points. He respected me from the start. He wanted me to discover my respect for him.

Seemingly all innocence, he asked me to fetch my husband. My head was spinning now. How had we got from water to husbands? I gave the familiar answer. But he wouldn't stop. He kept going. He knew me. He actually already knew me! How can you know someone when you've never met them? How can you know about five men and a sixth? How can you see into everything I hide? How can you get inside my guilt and my shame? How can you still be talking to me when you know too much about who I am?

I named him then, for the first time: a prophet. Only a prophet is going to know me like this.

We danced on together. I asked him about worship, the age-old dispute between Jews and Samaritans about where to worship properly. He took my ideas and stretched them again. He took history and started to rework it. He took the boxes we thought God lived in and broke them open. Real worship isn't about places, he said. Real worship isn't about styles or words or traditions or any dressing up. Real worship is about the spirit and about the truth. For as long as I can remember, I've wanted to know the truth. I've wanted to know the truth about myself and the truth about God. I've imagined how God must look at me and how much he must despair at what he sees. I've been afraid of that sort of truth. What if God rejects me too?

Could he be more than a prophet?

I named him again. The one we've all waited for, dreamed about, told endless stories about, begged God to send. The Savior. A good shepherd. A friend to hold us. A teacher to show us the way. A healer. One who could show us the ways of God. Messiah.

"I am he," he said gently. Three little words, and everything the world has ever wished for. "I am he." Three words to send the hunger away. Three words to defeat the shame. Just three words, and everything.

That's how he started to save me. Everything changed then. Part of it was simply that his friends arrived and instantly we were back in the old world of Jews and Samaritans, a woman on her own and a bunch of men staring at her.

Part of it was that I was a different person already. I think I started to know, there and then, what his living water might be. So, I ran back into the city and told anyone who would listen what was going on at Jacob's well.

People came. And they kept coming. For two more days he stayed with us. I think it freaked his friends out. But we were thirsty, we were so terribly thirsty. And he had what we needed, everything we needed, more than we ever deserved, more than we ever dreamed of.

By the time Jesus left us, we knew we had welcomed the Savior of the world. He had asked me for a drink of water on a hot day. But he had really come to let my life begin after so many years of drought.

And I have seen how others meet him still, all these years later. We know what happened in Jerusalem. We know how he died. We wept. And then we heard the rumors. Some of those same friends of Jesus came our way and told us. Risen from the dead! All our sins forgiven. Believe in him. Trust him still and always. Draw close to him by sharing bread and wine. Meet him in every moment of every day because the grave cannot hold him. Share his love with the world you meet. Trust him.

> "The water that I will give will become in them a spring of water gushing up to eternal life."[1]

---

1. John 4:14b

Lazarus

I REMEMBER ONE OF the stories Jesus told. It was about a man who had two sons. One demanded his inheritance and squandered it in a foreign land. Drought and famine came. The money and friends ran out and he ended up feeding pigs. That brought him to his senses. He packed up his pride and his arrogance and walked home, hoping that his father might take him on as a servant, hoping he might get a meal, knowing he was no longer a son. Meanwhile, the father had been watching for his lost son every day. He saw him in the distance, ran to greet him, flung his arms around him, kissed him, and wept over him. They held a great feast in honor of his son's return. Like so many of the stories Jesus told, it was the ending that did the hard work: "This son of mine was dead and is alive again; he was lost and is found!"

Jesus tells great stories. But the stories want to be much more than entertainment. He uses them the way a farmer uses a plow; to turn the ground over ready for the seeds. For him, the heart of everyone he meets is like that ground, rich and ready and waiting for new life. His stories set something moving inside us, prepare us to receive the seeds of hope and truth he shares.

I was lost, and he found me. He found all three of us, Mary and Martha and me. We heard about him long before we actually met him. Everyone did. I don't remember when, but he and his friends came through Bethany on their way to Jerusalem. Mary met them in the market and sat and listened. When he was finished, she asked him if he and his friends might want to share our table. That's where things began. We discovered that they had friends in many places who would offer them a bed and a meal as they passed through. We became a regular stop on his way over the Mount of Olives to and from Jerusalem.

We felt blessed. He showed us the things of God. He took my confusion and he understood my fears. I have tried to live well, kept the faith, followed the law, believed and trusted in God's ways. But I have had my demons. There are things I'm ashamed of, regrets and what-ifs that I can't let go. I have doubts. I've been hurt when God seemed to be so far away. As we got to know each other, he tilled all that soil with mercy.

I think many who meet him discover what it is to be lost and what it is to be found. Maybe they don't even know how lost they are until he shows them themselves. And that's where he does his best work. Our Scriptures and our prayers say plenty about judgment and salvation, about the ways God knows us and the ways God sifts and sees us. But with Jesus, somehow, these things came alive. Like that son, we could be as if dead even in our faith and he could bring us back to life.

Now, I hear that story differently. Lost and found. Dead and alive. All of it is true and all of it is me. I know that some are calling me "The Man Who Died." I suppose, for my remaining years, that will be my reputation. Mary and Martha, bless them, don't need to talk about it any more. We just try to live into this second chance at being a family. And it hasn't all been happy. Some think that I'm a curse, the product of sorcery, or a fake. They say that I was never truly dead. Some accuse me, with Jesus, of leading people away from God entirely. I've even been warned that my life might be in danger, just as his is. I'm bad evidence. I'm inconvenient. Part of me can't help but notice the irony, killing "The Man Who Died!"

My fever started as a cough I couldn't get rid of. It went on for days. Mary gave me all sorts of things to try to ease it. The neighbors gave us all their advice. A few in the village had contacts in Jerusalem and I went to see a physician. He gave me some powders to drink. They eased the pains a little and we thought the worst was over. But, after a night of sweating and shivering, I could barely move. It felt as if my body was getting heavier and heavier, as if just lifting my arm or turning my head took all I had.

I slept. I lost count of time. Mary and Martha never left me alone. They pressed cold cloth around me to try to cool me. They stroked my matted hair and talked and prayed. They pleaded and they begged. But I could barely whisper. They were hard to focus upon and I couldn't make out what they were saying. Everything slipped.

And then, nothing.

Or a dream, maybe.

It was not frightening. I remember a calm that seemed to grow, a peace.

Then there was light. And I could smell spices. My face was covered in something, and my arms were held by my side. I heard a bird singing. I felt a breeze. And then I heard the voice of Jesus call my name. He wanted me to come to him. It was a struggle to get up. Someone had bound my feet as well. All I could do was hop toward the light. As I did, my head hit rock. I staggered then. I think that was what finally woke me up and I knew where I was. I was in my tomb! They thought me dead!

I must have made a sound because I heard a crowd. Someone screamed. Then there were hands reaching for me, unwinding the bindings. They took the cloth off my face. Someone held out their hand to shield my eyes. I saw Martha and Mary. They ran. Their tears and mine overwhelming. We collapsed in a heap.

And, slowly, I became aware of Jesus. He knelt down in the dust with us. He put his hand to my cheek and I held it there as I shook. There were no words. The crowd was silent too. None of us could understand it. Or rather, only one of us. "Hello my friend," he said.

When the fuss died down a bit we were able to get to the house. Mary and Martha shooed everyone away. I think quite a few were happy to leave us to it because this was a fearful strangeness and they didn't want to linger. Slowly, I heard the story of how I died.

I had been dead almost four days. They had done all they could for me, but my life had ebbed away in the early hours one morning. Mary and Martha had washed me and prepared me. No wonder I could barely move; Martha is a devil with her knots! I was placed in the tomb and the stone had sealed it and I was lost once more. Their mourning had begun.

Jesus sat quietly listening to all of this. I saw the tears in his eyes. Martha took up the tale. She had met him when he got here. And she had hated him a little then. It had been days since they had got word to him that I was ill. They had told him that my death was near, and they had begged him to come that I might be healed. What was the point of a friendship such as ours if not to keep us safe? Why miracles for some and not for us? Couldn't he taste the fear? And that was when Jesus had turned even this catastrophe into a field ready for his plow. Another lesson. A lesson that had me at its heart. Resurrection and life.

There is plenty I cannot explain. I don't know why things have been as they are. His timing still baffles me and I'm not sure Martha has quite forgiven him. But I was lost, and he found me. I was dead, and he gave me life all over again.

Mary, Sister of Lazarus, and the Costly Perfume

DEATH VISITS EVERYONE, SOMETIME. So many have felt that knife cut away ones they love. So many have known that theft. We've mourned with our friends and helped our neighbors as they've observed the rites and entered into their grieving. But whenever we set the table for Jesus and his friends, and he and my brother hugged in greeting, death fled from our home again. We no longer need to talk about it. The questions and the answers have sort of run themselves dry, I guess. There's only so much that can be said, and even more that can't be.

His last visit before death came for him started like the others. He sent word ahead that he was coming for Passover and would stop for the night with us. We made ready. There was the usual chaos as they all squeezed into our home. And something else. We knew all about the pressure they were under. We were under it too. Lazarus was a bad sign for some, a walking reminder of a power that made them nervous or a deception they hadn't yet unmasked. We had heard some threats. We knew full well that Jesus heard plenty. Some wondered if he should even give up trying to get into Jerusalem this time. Folk were nervous. Some of the disciples looked uneasy just being on the Mount of Olives.

There was an atmosphere that no food or light could lift. Silences loitered. Lazarus was next to Jesus whilst Martha was serving. They had their heads almost touching, deep in quiet conversation. I was by the door, waiting with the wine. And then I saw a tear on my brother's cheek, and Jesus put his hand upon his shoulder. And Jesus looked up at me . . .

I put down the wine and slipped to the other room where the chest sat in the corner under the old woolen rug. Pulling the rug away, I heaved up the heavy lid and rummaged for a moment. The little alabaster jar lay wrapped in its soft leather. I untied the cord and felt its cool smoothness. It wasn't full any more. Martha and I had used some to prepare our brother for his burial not so many weeks before. The deep scent of the nard kept his decay at bay for a while; and the use of it was a symbol of the pricelessness of love. It was a family treasure, imported from far to the east and staggeringly costly. We had been keeping it as a final gift of love to one another when the time came for each of us to be buried. Martha had lifted it with trembling hands and brought it to where Lazarus lay. Jesus had undone our planning; not that we minded! Now, though, I knew it had another purpose.

As I went back to the meal, they were all deep in conversation. Martha was clearing some of the dishes and Lazarus was helping. Peter and Thomas were having some sort of argument and I could see Bartholomew listening to them with that half smile of his. Glancing up and seeing me, he winked and nodded at them both as if to say, "Same as usual."

Jesus was watching everyone, listening in, letting the space and the setting weave their magic. He seemed more relaxed now, enjoying this buzz and the jostling of friendship. As he lay on the cushions it was easy for me to settle by his feet. None of the others paid me much attention. They probably thought I was wanting to join the conversation as I had done in the past.

I opened the jar as it rested beside me. The rich amber oil was thick and sticky. I could smell its sweetness straight away; the scents of freshly cut wood mingled with spices and so many things. Jesus turned to watch me. I dipped my fingers, gently placed his foot in my lap, and started to rub the oil into his heel. As my touch warmed the nard it grew easier to work and I teased it up around his ankle and down toward his toes. Taking a little more, I rubbed and coaxed the nard between each toe, gently massaging each of them with fingers now rich in the perfume. Bending low, I kissed his foot softly as the scent enveloped me. My hair fell around my eyes and I let it enfold his foot, sticking slightly. I wiped his foot with bunches of my hair, caught up in a little world all of our own. Leaning back, I let go and Jesus drew his foot away and offered the other. I gazed into his eyes as he watched me, waiting. More nard, and the ritual began again; heel and ankle, the top and the sole, finally the toes. Another kiss and then my hair wiping and caressing. I sat back, my hair and hands sticky and sweet. "Bless you," Jesus said quietly.

I wasn't surprised that there was silence in the room. All eyes were upon us. Lazarus and Martha were standing together in the doorway. He nodded his understanding. Of all of us, he knew what the nard was meant for and all it signified. He understood the way in which death approaches and the possibilities of meeting it. He knew how those who face the death of one they love find ways to make a little bit of their hearts ready. We want to offer what we can, even when anything we do is like the blade of grass on the wind seeking to hold the storm at bay. We long to not be where we find ourselves, but love and faithfulness hold us in the place. We weep and fight and make ourselves busy until the truth finds its way again, and we must face it.

Somehow, in ways I could not then explain, I knew that Jesus was going to the city this last time so that the city could kill him. He had spoken so many times of the plans of God unfolding in the world; of truth and justice, love and kindness, welcome and abundance. He had taught us always of the hospitality of heaven and the ways in which Emmanuel brings God to us, closer than the beating of our own hearts, calming all our fevers. And he had told us that the Son of God had come to die, that this was his way.

So, I anointed him, made him ready, did my part. It was my goodbye and my thank you. It was, like so much, a little sign of so much more. It was my worship and my service. It was an offering. The perfume filled the room, heavy and evocative.

If Lazarus understood, Judas didn't, or didn't want to. He condemned my extravagance and waste. His grimness pulled at the mystery and trampled my devotion. But Jesus would have none of it. He knew the measure of things better than anyone. He accepted my gift for what it was. He knew the cost. He spoke of the burial ahead.

Suddenly, death was back and all too real; a threat filling the room as powerfully as the scent. Heads were being shaken and protests were muttered. Judas looked at me, his face grim. Martha was by my side. She reached down and picked up the jar, wiped it gently and sealed it once more. Then she took my hand as I stood. Jesus joined us in the corner of the room, his back to everyone else. He put his hands on our shoulders.

"I know," he said. "This is a beautiful thing."

5

Holy Week

A Woman Having Her Feet
Washed by Jesus

WITH PASSOVER APPROACHING, THE city was packed and noisy. The Romans were always more nervous at the festival and had soldiers checking the long lines of pilgrims as they came through the gates and crowded the markets. Rebecca and I had to go out early to avoid spending ages waiting to buy the last things we needed.

Jesus had often found a welcome with us. When he wanted to stay overnight in Jerusalem rather than walk back to Bethany, he would get word to us. He and some of his friends had celebrated Passover with us a few times. This year was going to be different though. Peter and John came and told us that Jesus wanted to bring all of the twelve. The upstairs room is large, but with our family as well it was going to be a squeeze! Seth and I carried up more mats and we hunted out all the cups and bowls we could find. Rebecca spent a long time at the market but finally came home with enough to let us offer them a proper meal. If he remembered, Judas might even give us something toward the cost!

As the sun went down and the lamps were lit, they all arrived. Jesus greeted us as warmly as ever. He had brought some wine with him. "A thank you," he said, as I took it from him. They made their way upstairs and Rebecca, Seth, and I got busy with the food and drink. Eventually, everyone was settled, reclining around the tables which now were laden. Rebecca had created a gorgeous display of figs and pomegranates surrounded by green almonds and walnuts as a centerpiece. The smells of the soup, lamb, and herbs and the cheery lamplight flickering across the faces filled the room with welcome. Conversations were spiced with laughter.

Seth took bread in his hands and said the prayer: "Blessed are you, Lord our God, Ruler of the universe, who brings forth bread from the earth." Reaching over to a cup of wine, he gave thanks for us all: "Blessed are you, Lord our God, Ruler of the universe, who creates the fruit of the vine." We shared a moment of silence. And then the conversation bubbled up once more as food and drink were passed around.

It was as the meal continued that Jesus got to his feet and went over to the water jars in the corner beside Rebecca. Assuming he wanted to wash his hands, Rebecca started to get up, but Jesus waved her away. He dropped his cloak on the floor and wrapped a towel around his waist. Then he poured some water into a basin and turned back toward the table. Most of us had noticed and were staring at him, wondering what on earth he was up to. Without a word, Jesus moved to the first pair of feet he could find. They belonged to Rebecca. He knelt down on the floor and, with great care, took her foot, held it over the basin, and cupped water over it. Jesus was washing our daughter's feet! He used the towel to dry them off and then, still on his knees, moved to the next one of his friends to start the whole ritual over again.

By now the room was silent and we could all hear the water as he splashed it on foot after foot. He came to me and smiled as he took my old feet with their callouses and corns and soothed them with the water and the gentleness of his touch. It was a slow process with him crawling round the room, shuffling the basin along the floor and taking his time to wash each one of us. There were looks of embarrassment and looks of surprise. A few giggled. Some shook their heads but let him take their feet anyway. He got to Peter. And it was Peter who said what most of us had been thinking. He protested that this was inappropriate. Jesus was demeaning himself by acting like a servant. If anyone needed to be the honored guest it was Jesus. So how could it be that the one we most respected was the one on his knees wiping the dust and grime and sweat from the feet of his friends?

Jesus promised that the strangeness of all of this would make sense eventually. Jesus tended to do that. It could be very infuriating! And then he told Peter something very odd: "Unless I wash you, you have no share with me."[1] "In that case," said Peter, "wash my head and hands too!" Peter always was something of a literalist! But Jesus shrugged him off, saying that enough was enough and that this foot washing was sufficient.

He moved on again, completing his circuit of the table and all the feet laid out on our mats. Getting back to Rebecca's corner, Jesus took off the

---

1. John 13:8b

towel and put on his cloak. Then he took his place again at the table. But now he was sitting up with his legs crossed. He clearly had things to say.

He asked us what we understood of what he had just done. Even as a few heads shook he answered his own question for us. He said that he wanted to show us a truth and leave us with an example to follow. It was another parable, but this time it was a parable of wet feet and a damp towel and a teacher on his knees. This time, Jesus was the story and so were all of us. He had taken on the task that we would assume belonged to the least important in order to open up to us how we should handle importance. If he was the one we named Teacher and Lord, then he was setting those titles free of any status or privilege and filling them instead with the heart of a servant and the commitment of love.

He went on to say many more things that night in our upper room. But I think it was this act that lives on for me just as he meant it to. It was both completely unexpected and utterly understandable at the same time. He wanted to get inside our thinking about the way things should be and offer us a better way. He wanted to surprise us the way his parables always offered surprise so that we would get caught in the strangeness of it all. And the truth would linger, become a little bit more real, precisely because he showed us what it looked like and how it felt. Jesus loved ideas and he loved words. But around that table, in the midst of our meal, he gave us more than words and ideas. He gave us his touch, his fingers between our toes, and the clean water washing the dust away. He gave us himself on his knees. He took off his power like he took off his robe and laid it down so that he could get closer to each one of us. He became all he spoke of. None of us knew, that night, just how far he was going to go to become all he spoke of.

It will soon be Passover once more, our first since he died and rose again and left us to live his way. Many of his friends have headed off across the land to tell the stories and share what he revealed. Some have lost their lives. Some have taken to hiding. John is going to join us for the feast. We'll be a much smaller household upstairs this time, gathered around that table. I know we'll remember many things. There will be tears. And there will be joy. Jesus was so much part of things that I still expect to hear him at the door, even though he told me such a time was passing. We'll have the table ready and welcoming. Rebecca will have been busy.

In the corner, as reminders of all he taught us of his new ways, we'll have a jug of water and a basin and a towel.

A Young Woman at the Last Supper

THERE'S A STILLNESS WHERE the talking was, a silence in this upper room. Everyone has gone. Mother and father are in bed downstairs. My sleeping mat is ready for me, unrolled beside the table. The bowl with the last of the pomegranates, figs, and nuts is still sitting where I placed it on grandmother's embroidered cloth. I've just kept the last lamp alight. Somehow, I don't want this night to end. So much has happened that I don't understand.

When Jesus and his friends came to share at our table again I was glad. It had been a while since he had stopped with us. We all got busy making preparations and I had to wait ages in the market to get fresh food. The pilgrims were making Jerusalem as busy and crazy as they always do. And the Romans were bossy and shouting. It was good to get home with most of the things we needed. By then, Peter and John were already upstairs shifting furniture and arguing about who would recline where.

The meal started, as they do, with father's prayers and blessings. I was near the door so that I could help when we needed to fetch anything. Jesus started to make tonight strange and special when he left the meal and washed my feet in front of everyone. But that's a different story. This story is about the meal Jesus changed.

He interrupted the meal to do some teaching. He often did that. I think he loves the way a meal makes everyone more ready to listen. But this time, he didn't take us on one of his journeys into Scripture or make up a story. This time, he scared us. He said that someone eating with him was going to betray him. It was shocking. People protested. Of course we did! Who amongst us would ever do anything to hurt him? We love him so much. I didn't understand it. I couldn't see how such a thing could happen. I knew there were people who didn't like him, who found him difficult and who said his words were wicked. But they didn't really know him the way we do. So, what was he talking about? I looked at mother; she was just staring at him.

Then, Jesus reached across the table and took up a loaf of bread. He said the blessing: "Blessed are you, Lord our God, Ruler of the universe, who brings forth bread from the earth." Jesus broke the loaf in half and offered it to Peter and James who were reclining on either side of him. They didn't know what was going on. And then Jesus said: "Take it and eat it; this is my body. Do this to remember me." James broke off a piece and passed the bread to Matthew. Peter was still just holding what he had, confused and uncertain. Jesus motioned to him to break some off and eat it.

As the bread was passed around the table in the silence, the room felt different. I've lived in this house all my life. But it felt like we were in a new and frightening place that I didn't know. When the bread reached me, I broke a tiny piece off and ate. And all the time I was trying to understand. What did Jesus mean? How could this piece of bread be his body? And why did he need to say we had to remember him? Was he going away? Where was he going?

He loved his parables and his signs and wonders. He loved always having another question. Was this another lesson? Was he making the meal, and us, into one of his parables? But he hadn't even finished. As my head was spinning and the bread was sticking to my teeth, he took up the cup and blessed it in the normal way as God's gift of the fruit of the vine. Then, holding it in both hands, he looked around us all and said we all needed to drink from this cup he had blessed. ". . . this is my blood of the new covenant, which is poured out for many for the forgiveness of sins."[1] The familiar meal, the easy conversations, the room I know, had gone by now. We were in a place none of us understood and none of us wanted: bread becoming the teacher's body, wine becoming his blood. I sat back against the wall, confused and frightened.

As we passed the cup around the circle and took a sip, Jesus watched. He wasn't smiling. Whatever this was, it mattered to him. Whatever he was trying to show us was important. The cup got back to him, and he emptied it. Very carefully, he set it down on the table beside the remains of the bread. He looked around, letting himself take in all of our faces and the difficulty we were sharing. "I tell you, I will never again drink of this fruit of the vine until that day when I drink it new with you in my Father's kingdom."[2]

1. Matt 26:28
2. Matt 26:29

It was my father who broke the spell and simply asked what all of us wanted to ask. What was going on? "You will understand when the time comes," Jesus said. "Don't you remember what I've told you on the road?" He was looking around at the others. Some just stared. One or two slowly nodded, averting their eyes.

"I told you that I must be betrayed. And I'll be handed over. They'll have their way with me. And they will kill me. But I've told you much more, haven't I. Dying isn't the end. Betrayal isn't the end. Denial doesn't destroy me. Three more days, and I promise you I'll rise and you'll see me again. This is how God's kingdom comes."

I had never heard any such things before. From the looks on their faces, neither had mother or father. It was like having someone punch you, hard. But there were a few more nods around the table. They had heard this before! They did know something! And this meal made strange was part of it, somehow.

And then, with all this awfulness in the room, Jesus started to sing. He sang softly. Slowly, reluctant and confused and scared, others joined in. I found myself singing. And the tears came:

> "The Lord is my shepherd, I shall not want.
> He makes me lie down in green pastures;
> he leads me beside still waters;
> he restores my life.
> Even though I walk through the valley of the shadow of death,
> I fear no evil;
> for you are with me;
> your rod and staff—
> they comfort me.
> You prepare a table before me
> in the presence of my enemies;
> you anoint my head with oil;
> my cup overflows.
> Surely goodness and kindness shall
> follow me all the days of my life,
> and I shall dwell in the house of the Lord
> my whole life long."[3]

3. Ps 23

Judas Iscariot

I HAVE DONE IT for all of you, can't you see? My brothers, I have played my part to the full so that we will be free.

Jesus always knew. He chose me for this. I remember our first meeting. Is it really three years? I was counting money when he came to my home, my own money and some I had liberated from others. At first, I thought they were simply passing by, another wandering rabbi with his brood of fools waiting for wisdom to fall on their heads. I'd seen plenty come through on their way toward their own particular wilderness.

But this group was different, somehow. He was different. They were this uneven mix of workers and fishermen, the educated and the less so. And there was the traitor, pretending not to see me. But I saw you right away didn't I, Matthew? Oh yes. We knew each other. I had kicked over your booth and beaten you senseless and would have cut your throat if your Roman minders hadn't come running at your screams. Fattening yourself on the poverty of our people. Betraying us every time your sweaty hands grab the coins and pass them on to the scum who think they own us.

I am Sicarii. We do not fear the fight that is coming. We long for it because it is the promise of freedom. I'd taken lives. Not as many Romans as I wanted to, but traitors and spies had met my blade in the dark. We were always few. But we could keep the sentries nervous every night. The stories about us helped feed the fear in those who deserved to be afraid.

And he knew all this. Jesus stood in my home, watching me staring at Matthew, and he knew my heart. My secret was never a secret from him. He looked into my eyes and my camouflage faded away like morning mist in the brightness of the sun. I was known for all I was, revealed in all my anger.

And then he asked me to join you.

Matthew ran, and we all heard him retching outside my door. "Something he's eaten?" someone wondered aloud with a smirk. I'm not alone in despising tax collectors. "Something to digest," Jesus replied. Then he told me you were staying in the town for another night, moving on in the morning. He told me where to find all of you if I wanted to.

After you all left, I sat and wondered. I didn't know what this meant. But slowly, it felt like a possibility. What better cover than to join a band of wandering students with their teacher? I would be able to travel unnoticed. Opportunities would come. My knife would find employment. My purse would find comfort. And I could keep in touch with my brothers; follow the secret signs and leave them word of Roman troops and weaknesses.

Next morning, I was in the square early. The look on Matthew's face was priceless. And things got even better, in those first few weeks, when Jesus put me in charge of the purse. I wondered if Matthew might just drop dead in the dust there and then out of shock and anger and shame. It was exquisite, as if Jesus was toying with him, dangling Matthew on the line and watching his past chew him up.

But the weeks passed and the months came and things changed for all of us. Matthew and I are not friends. But the hatred in me and the fear in him have melted into something nearer friendship. I still have to watch out when I'm dipping into the money because Matthew can do the sums and he watches where the coins go. But, slowly, we have found a way to live with one another, even to understand each other. The same goes for the rest. There are many now. The women and men who travel most along with Jesus, and all the others who seem to know him and have a room and a meal ready for him. We've got used to each other. We talk plenty and listen more. We have witnessed things none of us can explain. We have trembled as the angels have walked with us and the Spirit of God has worked wonders.

There is a change deep within me. I have come to love the teacher too. Sometimes, when he and I are walking and talking away from the others, we speak of revolution. He always pushes back when I dwell upon the fight that has to come. We have argued over and over about the history of our people and the choices made to fight for freedom and to save the name of God from shame. I know the stories of those who would not kneel, the ones who would rather die than accept humiliation. But Jesus always manages to twist us toward other stories; prophets and promises, silent revolutionaries winning the world with love. I chide his naivety. He challenges my anger. Often, these arguments end when he tells me that the time is coming when I will understand. He tends to end quite a lot of conversations that way. And, without doubt, his move on Jerusalem and his increasing public attacks signal the start of something new. We can all feel the change, the tension rising, the showdown approaching.

I wonder. Did he always know that his greatest opportunity would come this way? As I walk into the garden we know so well, did he always know that this would be the part I had to play? Around me I hear the men drawing their swords. Torches glow on their blades as we fan out and shadows are dancing amongst the olives. If Jesus has done as he's done so often, he'll be praying in the center where the trees create a peaceful space.

We have no idea how many may be with him, so I will greet Jesus with a kiss as I have done so many times. My part ends. His work will unfold as only he knows how. I am just the one starting the landslide with a pebble. He will bring down the mountains and bury Rome for ever. And we will be free.

The money is a bonus. The price upon his head will go to help those who suffer as the fight begins. Blood money is a tainted, evil tool. It will be cleansed as it pays the bribes, gathers the weapons and assures the safe houses are there. I will pocket what I need.

He will shape the future his own way. I know that. No agenda other than his own will ever move him. But he will unleash the power of God to set us free. He has worked to his plan and I help it to become. No wonder he was so determined to share Passover in Jerusalem even as many warned him away. There can be no better place than the holy city. There can be no better time than this festival. We gather like a hidden army. We remember that our people were slaves to another tyrant. But God heard our cries. The might of Egypt could not stop us. The angels fought for us. The seas dried up for us. And we were free!

In this garden, in this darkness, we light the flame that will burn for ever. I will be hated at first for the part I play. But he has given me my orders. I am Sicarii. I obey.

The High Priest's Servant Girl

"Fetch more water."

"Bring the extra blankets and prepare an extra bed."

"Make sure the cleaning's finished in good time for Sabbath."

My life is all about getting things done without being noticed. I'm always in the background, silent and busy. I know how to keep the water jars filled and where they must be kept, ready and waiting. When the time comes for lighting the lamps, I'm always able to have them burning for the mistress even before she settles. When the cold of night creeps into our bones, I'll have the fire burning bright and the extra furs laid out. I know the importance of the rituals, how to keep things clean and how to avoid the unclean.

My family were proud that I was taken on by Caiaphas. They've looked after me, too, at the house of the High Priest. I am in as safe a place as anyone could be. The Romans tend to keep their distance, at least most of the time. They don't want to get mixed up in things that could lead to bigger trouble. They may not understand us, but they know enough to leave the priesthood alone as much as they can.

That week, things were happening. The house was even busier than the festival normally made it. Lots of conversations behind closed doors. Groups coming and going at all hours. More temple guards were stationed at the gates than I had seen before. We were constantly busy, fetching food, keeping the water jars filled, guessing who might need a space to sleep as the evening wore on.

That particular night, I remember, was really cold. The sky was clear and the stars were bright. We lit all the fires in the house and those outside gathered around the courtyard bonfires trying to find some warmth. A big meeting was happening. Many priests and officers had arrived, and it looked like the whole council was in session.

I was shooed away. They didn't want me getting under anyone's feet. The adults always get more strict as they get more busy! So, Becca and I found a space near one of the fires beside the gates with Joseph the gardener and his boy. Becca is my best friend. We always played together growing up in Bethany. She started at the big house before I did because her parents know the High Priest's wife. But they put in a word for me and that's how I was taken on. We sat and talked and poked sticks into the fire to make it send sparks up into the night.

Suddenly, a whole gang of men came down the steps and headed for our gate. We got out of their way as they lit their torches from the fire, grumbling about the cold. The firelight glinted off the spears and most of them had swords at their belts. Then they headed off into the dark and we settled back by the fire. Becca and I snuggled under a blanket.

I think I was asleep when the men returned. They were marching together, some torches still burning, swords at the ready. And, amongst them, his hands tied and being pulled along so that he had to almost run to stop falling over, was the rabbi from Galilee. Jesus. We all knew him. He was a regular speaker in the Temple courts. And he was trouble. Sometimes the master and mistress would keep talking about him as I worked around them. They spoke of his insults, of how he taught falsely, of how he was stirring people up and inviting chaos, or worse. The guards pulled him up the steps and into the house and the other men settled themselves around the courtyard, waiting and watching. There wasn't much talking now.

One or two stragglers gathered at the gate. There were quick conversations and then a couple of men came through. They looked around, saw a space at our fire, and joined us. Although they kept their heads down, we could hear their quiet conversation, hear the strong accents. Galileans.

Joseph went to get more wood for the fire. As he did so, one of the men shuffled out of his way and looked up. I knew that face! He was one of those who had been with the rabbi in the Temple during the week. He had said hello.

"You're with Jesus too, aren't you." I said. It wasn't a question. I don't know why I said it. It just came out.

"I don't know what you're talking about," he answered. He was up on his feet then, moving off into the darkness on the far side of the courtyard, avoiding people. His friend watched him go and drew his cloak tight. "I'm sure he was," I said to Becca. She nodded.

Later, we were taking food to the guards at the gate. Becca nudged me and pointed. There he was, the mystery man we both agreed was one of the followers of Jesus. She had recognized him too, spotted the accent. Why was he here? Was he going to try something crazy? Turning to the guards, Becca said that he was with the rabbi. Hearing her, the man shook his head and swore harshly. "No." The guards didn't know what to do. How could they believe two girls? "We'll watch him," they said. The man stared us down.

We got more busy then. The courtyard was filled with men gathered around fires and they all wanted food and drink and blankets. Some came and went into the house. The lamps stayed lit through the night. When they were low, we replaced them with fresh oil.

It was whilst I was filling a lamp that the man hurried past me again. He was being followed by a little group who were arguing. One of them called out to him, "Of course you're with him! Why else would a Galilean be here this night?" The stranger turned on them, angry now and cursing. "I do not know the man!"

The cock crowed.

I remember when my brother died, and news came to my father. You could see the agony creep into his face, see him crumbling before the howling began. That's what I saw now as this mystery man held his hands over his ears, like he was trying to shut the world out. All his anger vanished. Instead, there was horror. Spinning round he ran, pushing past the guards and out through the gate into the early dawn, his cloak flying behind him.

"Told you," someone said.

Pilate's Wife

I ALWAYS LOVE IT when we come to the residence in Jerusalem. I know the city is a dangerous place, especially at Passover. We've been in Judea long enough to know the threat of revolution that rises when the pilgrims swell the streets and the mood turns nasty. This festival of liberation throws a challenge our way. Slaves walking into freedom comes round like an annual invitation to defiance. Most people keep the feast without going overboard. But there are always some who will incite and dangle dreams. The garrison is strengthened and all of us are cautious. The spies earn their pay in times like this, making sure the legionaries pick some up before they can do their worst. Herod and his soldiers are as watchful as we are. The stakes are high for them too. The priests play their part in keeping things quiet.

Pontius feels the pressure. We've friends in Rome with Tiberius, but enemies too, plenty of them. A blood bath in Jerusalem would get us noticed in the wrong ways. The empire doesn't worry about the force he's used to keep the peace as long as he keeps a lid on things. But fanatics are bad for revenue. They take risks. They find something divine in rebellion. So, the Passover stretches long and hard for him and the garrison. Our servants get edgy. We want to get this over for another year. They spend ages in planning where to post the troops, looking for the likely flash points and avoiding the darkest alleys where a quick knife can find a throat.

He thinks it strange that I still love coming to Jerusalem in spite of it all. He would prefer that I stay safe in the palace with the gorgeous trees and lake at Caesarea Maritima. But I always come with him. We've faced worse in our service.

I fell in love with this city the moment I saw it on its hill. It reminds me a little of Rome when you get up close to the heart of it. The way the narrow streets suddenly run up to the magnificent walls of the temple and the palaces take me back to home. I have to stay in the praetorium of course;

going out without full guard and preparation invites kidnap or worse. But our windows give me the best views of the sunlight on the ancient stones, especially as they turn to pink and peach in the sunset. Some angles let me see the massive blocks of the new temple, clean and fresh and a little bit of glory in a forgotten province. We've a beautiful courtyard garden where the dates hang low and the gifted local gardeners keep the flowers blooming even in the driest days. There's a pool I sit beside often, the marble cut with a golden mosaic of vines swirling round the water.

I've made friends in Jerusalem. Some serve us when we are in residence here. Others see us on the coast when duties or business bring them westwards. We have to be careful about the people we get close to, of course. There are many who look to gain any possible advantage over us. You always guard the reputation. You always play the game. But I know the importance of friendship, and there are elements in the culture of this place and this ancient city that I treasure. I keep some of that to myself, though.

Maybe this is why my dreams started. Perhaps it was this place speaking when I began to wake up in the night, cold and trembling. So many ghosts and spirits. So much story. So much threat. So much glory.

That night, I was restless and barely slept. That day dawned bright and promised to be stifling. I felt unwell and, after briefly trying to eat, returned to my chambers. Pontius had already been busy. A crowd was gathering at the gates, noisy and restless. The soldiers were out in force with more waiting in the shadows. Staff were whispering in the corridors. I think I must have slept a little more.

The dream was terribly vivid when I woke up. It haunted me. I saw a man, a Jew, standing trial. Pontius was on the judgment seat. He was silent whilst the indictment was being read. This Jew was an enemy of peace. He was a bandit dressed up as a sage, a rebel hiding behind pretty words. He was out to start a fight with Herod and with us. He had too many followers to be ignored. He even claimed to be divine!

The clamor rose and rose and then the real danger came into view: "If you let him go you are no friend of Caesar."

Pontius has often sat in judgment. He is not afraid of what it takes to keep the empire strong and the peace lasting. He has watched how a rebellion can begin. He has stopped some, and been rewarded. He knows what it is to hold the lives of others in his hands. He uses the tools of diplomacy and he uses the tools of justice. He'll punish when needs be. Some call him cruel. I know him to be careful. And he is always careful of how things will look in Rome, where the real power lies.

In my dream, this lonely Jew was like the center of the wheel, the still point around which all else was turning. For all the danger and the threat, he stood quiet in his chains, his head held high, his eyes fixed upon my husband. He was already bruised and bloody, and yet he was the one who seemed to own the space and rule this trial. My husband might be holding his life in his hands, but that seemed not to matter to this prisoner. It was Pontius who was being judged, and judged by the very man who stood in chains before him.

I understood. This man knew the truth. All the accusations being made were false and fiction. He was being set up. He was innocent. To have him killed would be a crime. And the death of this one Jew would be a stain we could not wash away. He was a threat in ways the crowd could never understand, a threat to Pontius and to me and all we had tried so hard to build together. His execution would ring so loud in Rome that we would hear it, and it would become the signal for our own defeat.

My own shouting woke me up. A servant came, worried at my noise.

I could not let my husband fall into this disaster. I told Ruth what she had to do, making sure she could repeat the message word for word. I sent her off to find Marcellus. He would know how best to get word to the governor even if the trial had begun.

Alone again, I stared out of the window as the noise of the city rumbled on and the heat grew. In the distance, the sky was darkening.

Barabbas

LET ME TELL YOU, friend, about another prison I once knew, years ago. It was in Jerusalem, a dungeon deep beneath the Roman palace. If you were there in the winter the nights would chill you. If they held you in the summer the heat would burn your throat. The cells were big enough for a dozen or more to be held, chained at the ankles to each other and then secured to iron set solid and unbending in the walls. Too much movement had your neighbor cursing you or worse. So, most of the time, everyone would sit against the walls, sometimes talking, often silent. A tiny opening high up let in some light, but you existed mainly in the gloom or dark. The place stank of human filth and despair. What food there was was fought over. The strong survived long enough to hear their sentence.

I was there for treason. A rebel and a murderer. In the run-up to Passover, before the garrison was reinforced and the city went crazy with pilgrims, a few of us had taken our chance to make a bid for freedom. Herod Antipas was already in Jerusalem. This was our moment to strike him a blow that would topple him and his henchmen. We had agreed a time when we would hit the royal palace itself. If we could do enough damage fast enough, we could swing the people behind us and have Herod humiliated. Then the Romans would see that their puppet was a liability. We had people inside the court who knew where the weapons were kept and how the watches were arranged. There came a moment each night as the guards were changed when a silent attack could wreak havoc. If we could raid the armory and kill some along the way, we could turn our few into many and our silence into a roar that would deafen the king and get noticed in Rome. We all had our stories of brutality and extortion to tell. We all hated Herod and what he stood for. We all were prepared to die.

What went wrong? What went wrong was that we trusted, and we were betrayed. We got into the palace as planned and laid a few of the guards out as we did so. But as we approached the storerooms, suddenly a whole troop appeared from the shadows where they had been waiting for us all along. The fighting was brief. We were outnumbered. I took a spear in this leg which still makes me limp. The beatings killed two of my friends before they threw us into the cells.

The next day we were moved. Herod wanted our crimes to be heard before Pilate. He wanted us made examples of. He needed the Romans to show that they were the ones whose power had his back. That's how I got to know Pilate's prison.

The Romans have great skill in the ways to inflict pain. They can do it to your body, and they can do it to your mind. They wanted to know how many more of us were plotting and they did what they could to get it from us. But if you know you are going to die anyway, torture no longer has so much power. And if the lies you tell sound convincing, and are hard enough to verify, you buy yourself a little time to gain enough strength to face the next treatment. So that's what I did, what we all did. We lied, and we waited to die.

It was early when I first saw him. He was bound and lying in the courtyard when they brought me up from the cell. Roman soldiers were milling around. They marched us both up the stairs and out onto Gabbatha, the place of judgment, that pavement where so many have heard their end. Pilate was sitting on his bench, surrounded by guards and officials. He looked uneasy; a powerful man who didn't seem to have as much power as he wanted. There was a crowd. They were restless.

Pilate stood up and came forward until he was close to us. Our guards pulled the ropes hard, pinning our hands against our sides, the binding cutting. Several had their swords ready, nervous and watchful. This was a storm they were dancing with. Fire and fury and a force they were trying to contain.

Pilate called out my name. And then he said the name of this other man. Jesus. I had heard stories but never met him. He didn't look like much of a threat to the empire. The contrast between the two of us couldn't have been more stark. He the rabbi, me the fighter. He the teacher whose reputation was of gentleness and peace, me the revolutionary with blood on his hands and hate in his heart. How could it be that we ended up here, together, our lives held in Pilate's sweating palm?

My choices have always been my own. No one had forced me to do what I'd done. This was my road, and if Roman execution was its destination then so be it. They were risks I was more than ready to take, and would take again given a chance. Freedom is worth living for so it has to be worth dying for. I had seen too many lives wasted and ruined, too much corruption, too many insults. Pilate would have me crucified and I would shame them as they did it by the dignity I would show. Who knew, perhaps my death might even spark yet more rebellion? Let them kill me and try to stop the ideas! Freedom has always needed its martyrs.

But this other? This Jesus from Nazareth? How could a holy man make so many so afraid?

There was a custom, useful sometimes depending on your point of view. A prisoner might be released to soothe tempers as Passover approached. What an irony! Our festival of freedom from slavery in Egypt being launched with a prisoner set free by the empire that ruled us. It was a little symbol of mercy from the Romans who had more than enough prisoners already. It meant nothing to Pilate. It might make some family, somewhere, grateful. It might even distract a few. It didn't fool most of us.

Pilate called it out. Who should he release? Who did people want? Who got to live?

I was ready for it. I stood as tall as my ropes would let me. I stared out across their heads and saw the skyline and the deep blue of the sky, saw the birds wheeling. I stood tall and proud and undefeated. I would go to Golgotha and they would know they had not broken me. I would defy them to the end, never beg, never waver, never accept. I would die and this rabbi would go free. Let him teach and let his followers learn. My lesson would be the greater one, written against the blue on an imperial cross.

"Barabbas," they were shouting.

I know, it still does not make sense.

Jesus and I looked at each other. We said nothing, but doomed men have little conversation. I was in shock, too stunned to move. He just stood there, holding himself with dignity too; unbroken, just as I had planned to be. He nodded.

Then they pulled at my ropes and led me away. Pilate was washing his hands, drying them on a towel offered by a servant. The guards took me back down the stairs.

I heard how he died. Many have heard of it. Many claim more. I don't know. But as I face another night in this cell with all of you, I remember his face on that morning when he was chosen, and I was free. And still I wonder why.

Simon of Cyrene

IT WAS ALL ABOUT weakness, and it was all about power. The power was simple. Roman soldiers grab you, haul you out and swear at you, abuse you for the darkness of your skin. They jostle you as their officer shouts orders. They spit into the dust and push you round to the back of the party making its way from the city gate. I remember the officer, looking bored, leaning back in the saddle and watching me as if I was just some vaguely interesting insect. How they love the power, the Romans. How they love the way they can make us drop everything at a whim. Life and death they hold in their hands, and we all know it. Power without mercy.

It was a death march I had fallen upon.

I had arrived just the day before, after nearly three weeks on the road. The synagogue had sent me with their blessing to celebrate Passover in Jerusalem for the first time in my life. I had found our friends and settled in, visited the synagogue of the freed and been delighted to find other Cyrenians there. I was starting to learn my way around but had somehow ended up lost and wandering and unsure of how to find my way home. Before I knew what was happening, I found myself pressed against the side of the road, hemmed in with strangers and watching in spite of myself. That's when they picked on me.

The weakness in him was heartbreaking.

The other two were bruised and broken. Of course they were. But at least they still had the strength to carry the crossbeams over their shoulders. Their chains rattled and we could hear them breathing hard. Yet some deep obstinacy, some final defiance, gave them the strength to stumble on.

Not him.

He came last, virtually pulled along by two soldiers. One was by his side, softly mocking him, pushing him as he tried to hold the wood across his shoulders. The other, a huge man, held a rope tied around the criminal's waist. He would let it slacken for a moment and then tugged hard, enjoying the stumbling and the lurching. These two were intent upon humiliation. Contempt radiated from them like the stench of a corpse.

We watched, horrified and enraged and ashamed at our impotence.

It seemed inevitable. His wounds were bleeding through his gown. Someone had pushed a ring of thorns hard down upon his head and the blood was running with the sweat. He looked as if they had already beaten him half to death. He tottered, and the thick wood fell sideways from his shoulder to smack into the ground, catching the heel of one of his guards. The big man slapped him hard in the face and he fell.

I didn't catch what the soldiers said. Their officer was shouting from his horse and the other prisoners halted in their tracks, heads down. Then the shorter one was quickly eyeing the crowd and spotted me. He grabbed me, pointed to the beam and gestured that I was now the one who had to carry it. What else could I do?

I stepped over him as he still lay, gasping in the dust. I knelt and took hold of the rough wood. I felt the splinters. It was heavy, but not impossibly so. I stood up slowly, settled it across my shoulders and stepped backwards to make room for him to stand.

"Get up," I prayed. "Please, get up. Don't let them finish you here, like this."

The big Roman grabbed him by his arm and hauled him to his feet. He swayed, but moved off, one foot slowly finding the ground after the other. I saw the blood on his heels.

We made our way. The silent crowd stepped back as we passed. I was aware of people crying. Someone called a name, softly. Another threw a flower that soon was trampled. Others spat at the condemned. Perhaps they knew what they had done. Perhaps these three deserved their punishment. Maybe they had innocent blood on their hands. I remembered the stories of robbers on the road and thieves in the night. I had heard of a family left to die in the wilderness by men who did not care at all.

On we went. The sun was higher now, and hot. There was a constant buzz of flies. We were no longer in the shadows of the city walls. The road was rocky and uneven. Dust caught in my mouth as I hauled my burden and watched my feet so as not to trip. I didn't want to be trapped in this any longer than I had to. The smaller Roman was behind me. I could hear his leather creaking as he walked. Just ahead of me, still being pulled along by the other guard, the man about to die was still stumbling. But, free of his weight, he was managing to stand a little taller. The officer's horse lifted its tail and we stepped around the dung and the cloud of flies.

It took me a moment to realize that the crowd had stopped walking with us. They were hanging back now, a silent audience to the destruction to come. I heard later what they named the place: Golgotha. Death had found its home beside the holy city. All rock and dirt and the stuff of nightmares. More soldiers were already there, chatting as they waited. They, too, fell silent as we approached. Five sturdy posts, taller than a man, stood wedged into the rocks, stained and cut from previous crucifixions. The Romans only needed three that day. They had ladders up. I heard the nails rattling in a bucket. The officer on his horse gave some orders and the three prisoners were herded to one side. The two who had carried their crossbeams dropped them. The third fell to his knees and sat back. I knelt beside him as the big Roman grabbed the wood and dragged it from my shoulders, grating the skin on my neck.

I was catching my breath when I realized that the prisoner had turned to look at me. His face was streaked with sweat and dust and blood. His eyes held mine, lingering. "Thank you," he mouthed.

I had no words.

All I could manage was the briefest of nods as I stepped away, stepped back and tried to put distance between myself and the scene about to unfold. One of the Romans had a jug and a cup. He went from prisoner to prisoner, offering them the drink. The one whom I had helped took a sip, then shook his head. One of the other condemned men was pulled to the ground, his arms outstretched across the plank that he had carried. A hammer glinted in the sunlight.

Mary, the Mother of Jesus, after the Crucifixion

THE WHISPERING TELLS ME that they are still awake and hope that I might be sleeping. But how can I sleep? This vision of my son keeps rising up to suck the life out of me. The sea of tears has run dry. My throat burns. I am trembling again despite the blankets.

They are kind. Their goodness wants so much to take me in and make me safe. I know they mean so well. They simply want to do what he told them to do. They want to take the place of my firstborn son; make their home my home. Keep me safe. And it is hard for them as well. They loved him too. They shared so much, hoped for so much more. They left lives behind like so many to follow him. They tasted the risks and the uncertainties. Awkward questions. Accusations and mockery. They believed so strongly. I know their hearts are broken too. I know.

But I am his mother!

I *was* his mother.

Will I ever get used to that? Does this ever become possible, this change from present to past? Will I breathe again without choking?

My son! My son. My son.

The memories come without me looking for them. Ancient Simeon's words are haunting me now. When Joseph and I presented you in the Temple, he took you in his arms and sang a salvation song. He said you would build up and tear down. And, as he handed you back to me, he touched my cheek and whispered that my soul would bleed because of you. I had already dipped into those waters. Then, I thought I had outlived his prophecy when we fled into Egypt and had to hide. I thought it again at times as you grew up and the strange things happened and as you did what sons can do to their mothers. I thought it when you left to begin these years on the road, when the stories came of the risks you were taking and the storm you were conjuring. But to listen to you hang . . .

Simon, I think it was, who brought the news. I don't remember. Confusion and darkness and you in chains somewhere. Betrayal. And all of a sudden it was the Romans. We knew what that meant. Pilate held the power of life and death. That's when hope died in me. If you were in front of Pilate, you were bringing about the end you had spoken of. That man loves cruelty, and he loves to make examples of those he can. Mercy is his stranger. You had been speaking of dying. You even said it in my hearing and you knew what that was doing to me. Some told me you knew it would be Pilate and you said it would be the cross.

I had no need of the frantic arguments some were having yesterday. Schemes to get you out. Talk of bribes. So and so is a guard who could be useful. I knew all of it was pointless, the desperation of the foolish. I knew you too well to think you hadn't calculated these final moves. If you wanted to save yourself, you would. You had done it before. Angry people had let you slip through their fingers without even knowing they were doing so. You made yourself scarce when you felt the time wasn't right. You could summon adoration, wrap yourself in crowds that even the Romans would be fearful of. In God's name, you could summon the armies of heaven!

Of course you could.

But you wouldn't, would you? Not now. Not with this Passover. Not with Pilate. Not with things done and yet to be done.

No.

I didn't need anyone to help me understand when the word came that they were bringing you out. I covered my head and left. Some of the others joined me. Both Marys, silent, walked with me. A few of your disciples. I don't blame the others for their fear. I don't think my soul had room to be afraid. Or rather, there was nothing left in me to feel beyond the abyss.

We followed at a distance, behind the crowd who themselves lingered at the edge of things, away from where the soldiers and their prisoners dragged along. I sometimes saw your head. I saw you go down, several times. I saw another man take up the crossbeam. Mary held me close when the screaming began and the murmur lifted from the crowd as other mothers joined the cries. I heard the hammers. My God!

Then the ropes went tight and the soldiers on the ladders grappled with bodies slippery with sweat and blood. And, in the middle of the three, there you were, rising. Head dangling, a ring of thorns falling. I remember the wind blowing and dust. It takes time. The Romans sat and diced whilst their officer on his horse drank. Some of the crowd drifted away and suddenly there was no one between me and you. I saw you, fully saw you, for the first time. I sat there then, sat in the dust and hugged my knees close and stared up at you. Others were with me still. Someone had an arm around my shoulders. Someone was weeping.

I did not want to watch. But I could not take my eyes away, not for a moment. If this was all that I could do, if this was the only thing left to me, I wanted to make sure that the last face you saw was mine. I pulled my scarf off and let the wind blow the hair from my eyes. And the tears came then. It was as if the air grew thin and I had to gasp it in, great gulps that shook my body and left me spitting out dust as my eyes filled. I kept wiping my face.

You lifted your head a little, opened bruised eyes, stared into mine. You did not mouth a word and nor did I. What word could we? On it went, that day hauling itself into darkness.

Later, you looked again. And that was when we heard you say that I was adopted by your friend. I was to go with them, and they were to take me in. This was how you fulfilled your duty. Even at the end, you were making something new. Your blood brothers and sisters were not to be the ones whose homes would be mine. Instead, amongst those whom I only met because of you, would be a place for me.

You asked for a drink.

And then you died.

We stayed for a long time. By the end it was just a few soldiers and the families of the dead. One or two friends maybe. I saw them take you down. I held you then, both of us shattered and ruined. Finally, they took you from me and brought me here. They wanted me to eat something.

Now I wait as this night turns and everything burns.

Joseph of Arimathea

WE DID ALL THAT we could. It was the last and it was little, but it was something. At least we gave him back a fraction of the dignity he was robbed of. As this holiest of days dawns, I can give thanks for that.

It surprised me, to be honest, the way Pilate let us claim him. And we surprised ourselves as we gave such publicity to the claims Jesus had upon us. I had stood away as the council made its choices. The arguments had some merit. Jesus was certainly a disturber. His actions were as provocative as those of any prophet. And the dividing line between holy prophet and dangerous rebel can be as thin as parchment. I made my disquiet clear, whilst being careful not to declare too much. I didn't know, then, exactly where I stood. He had touched me with his wisdom and the winsome ways in which he let our traditions and teachings arc always toward generosity and justice. He could be partial in the texts he quoted, but his answers had a power and a conviction that could be captivating. I heard him often. We talked a few times. He would tell me that I was not far from the kingdom, and I would ask him what more was needed. "Follow me," he would say. Follow me. So much to hang upon so small a command. Too much.

Things moved faster than I had expected, faster than most of the city knew. Even as the first fires of the day were being lit, Jesus was already in with the council. That he was taken to the governor was inevitable. It was all part of the debates we had been having. In this fragile festival, when so much passion simmered, only a Roman intervention would keep things in proportion. The last thing we needed was a riot and another bloodbath. But his followers, trailing him into the city and gathered with him in the Temple, seemed more confused than confrontational. Their fears and disorganisation were part of our gamble.

I could not bear to be there as the end came. I stayed away. Many did. The women shamed us with their devotion and their boldness. I heard that his mother had stayed, along with some of the others. But most of us made ourselves scarce.

As yesterday drew onwards there was a stillness that seemed unnatural, as if even the birds had lost their voice. I stayed in, trying to pray and wondering what to pray for. If he truly was the Messiah, shouldn't this be the moment when all was revealed? Would fire fall from heaven? Would the angel of death shatter the legion? Would we come face to face with the power of the Almighty? And if we did, where would I be? Was I numbered with the righteous or counted with transgressors? Was my ineffective dissent anything more than a cloak to hide my own shame and complicity in the death of an innocent man? Would I be found guilty? On and on and on!

By noon, it seemed that God truly was on the march. What seemed to be a storm became a tent of darkness falling upon Zion. We had to light the lamps. People cowered. The animals pulled and the dogs were barking. It lasted for three terrible hours. How often, then, I longed for Arimathea! To be anywhere but here. To have any other life than the life that trapped me and the doubts that haunted me.

Then came the word. Dead! I met some of the council in the street, coming from the place. There was no jubilation and no relief. They had watched him to the end, watched as the sky threatened and the inevitable drew closer. They heard his screams, and they heard him say the Psalm. Truly, he was godforsaken at the end. So much hope dying with him. So many dreams turning to dust. "Follow me," he said. Where to, Jesus? Where to?

The Passover Sabbath was approaching. I thought of him hanging there, naked upon his cross amidst the filth of Golgotha. I thought of the things done to him to break his body. I felt the shame. I thought of the times we had spoken and the way he had treated me; respectful even in his challenging. And a thought came; a longing for a tiny piece of dignity in this catastrophe. Maybe it was as much my shame as my devotion. Maybe that's why others joined me. We needed to rescue something, even if just our own humanity.

Pilate is a brute of course. But he isn't stupid. He has been here long enough to know that, sometimes, letting a tradition take over can be helpful. We let him know that we wished to exercise the normal practices of burial. Word came that this would be permitted. The order was sent to Golgotha. We would not be prevented. In fact, by the time we got there, the Romans already had their ladders up to aid us. The two who had been crucified with Jesus were also being taken down; family and friends with the same task we had and as anxious to see a final lawful act dignify their deaths. In the midst of all of this brutality, in this place of execution, some gentleness refused to die. Faith might still be honored.

We had linen and spices, gathered in haste, and laid them out upon the ground. We stood beneath him. His feet, cold and bloodied, were at the height of my waist. I reached out and felt the nail. Two others climbed up on either side of him. I worked at the nail until it came free and cradled his feet as the wood gave him up. They undid the ropes around his arms and pulled the nails. Slowly, gently, straining under his weight and fearful he might fall, we lowered him to the ground and rolled him onto the sheet.

We covered his face quickly.

We wiped what we could away and cleaned him as best we could whilst the guards looked on and a few of his closest sat weeping. His mother held him long, her tears wetting the linen and mingling with his blood. With the spices we had we anointed him. The myrrh must have been the only pleasing fragrance to fill the air of that place that day.

The three of us did not find him too heavy as we wrapped the cloth as tightly as we could and lifted him from the ground. A nod from the Romans and we were free to go. We felt his mother's anguish burn against our backs.

The path led down toward the side of the valley. We stopped on the way to rest. We had no need of talking and no words to share. It was peaceful. No one passed us. I was aware that the women were following, taking their time, silent too and watching. The rock rose hard beside the path where a few trees grew to cast their lengthening shadows as the day drew on. We had to watch our feet to keep from stumbling. We passed some tombs, their entrances bricked up. One had an ancient and broken lamp amidst the stones and signs of a fire where some family had stayed to mourn.

We came to the tomb I had arranged. It was not much, just a tiny chamber gouged into the rock. The entrance was so small and low that only one of us could enter at a time. We passed the body of Jesus through and laid him on the sand. I folded a cloth to place under his head on the shelf. We lifted him then, and set him to his rest. We spoke the words of the prayers. And we left him.

6

Easter

Mary Magdalene on Easter Morning

Slip out into the darkness before anyone is moving. In my bag, the ointments and the spices bought in the market in the last moments of the Day of Preparation.

Jesus was dead by then.

To end that life!

To bring him down and smash him as they did. To meet his love with so much cruelty. To hang him high. So much of myself died then . . .

He meant everything. From the first time I heard about him and the first time I met him, he gave so much to me. He had spent time with us in the village, teaching amongst the boats, laughing with some of the fishermen, watching the sunset across the Sea of Galilee. They took me to him, me with the demons toying and dancing. I screamed as he turned toward us. I wanted to run. Everything in me wanted to run. But he was smiling. Not the smile of the men who laughed at me so often. Not the cruel smiles that have plagued me. Not the name-calling smiles. His was gentle, kind, welcoming, real. He reached out his hand, touched my shoulder. "Hello Mary." And that was all it took. His greeting was enough. He knew me long before he met me, knew the torments within me, and he cast them out. People said I had seven demons. There and then, he chased them away with his gift of welcome. Such a peace as I had not known. So much love.

That was years ago. I've loved him and helped him ever since. When I could, I would get food and fresh clothes to him and his friends. Whenever my cloth trade was good, and money was spare, it went into their common purse. Sometimes, they would eat with us if they were passing through on one of their travels around Galilee. As another Passover approached and he spoke about going to Jerusalem, I joined them on the pilgrimage.

It turned into a nightmare.

What began with joyous celebration as we processed him down from the Mount of Olives swung toward something deathly all too quickly. We could sense it. He was picking fights in the Temple, speaking hard words sometimes, almost goading. Opposition felt strong; there were huddles of angry faces amongst the listeners. Romans all over the place. The city felt frightened and frightening. We had the use of a home in Jerusalem and gathered in the upper room to eat with him. Several of us joined the family. We heard Judas leaving. Jesus took some of them out into the night as he went to the garden to pray. They were gone a while and then we heard running and people were pounding on the door. They tumbled in, breathless and petrified. They managed to tell us about the arrest. Soldiers and temple guards, Judas leading them, the beginnings of a fight and then Jesus calmly letting them take him away. Simon was missing too.

Rumors then. All sorts of rumors. We didn't know what to do. We waited for news when there wasn't any. We talked about what to do next but didn't dare. So, we kept the doors shut and prayed. Finally, Simon appeared. He was broken, despairing. Silent. News reached us of a trial. Some said that Jesus would be all right. Remember storms and angry crowds? He'll walk through this one too. But he didn't, did he.

No. This time there wasn't going to be a miracle. By the time we saw him, dragging the crossbeam, he was beaten. It made no sense. We had seen what he could do, how the impossible hovered around him and the ways he could change hatred and anger into love. I knew. I knew his power. He had saved me by casting out the demons that tortured me. He had given me life again. He had lifted me from all my suffering. Why not himself?

That day refused to end. Even the mob felt the agony of it all. Some drifted away. Others whispered. Some wept. The four of us sat in the dust, clutching one another, watching as they diced for the clothes we had patched and washed. I had my arms round Mary as she trembled. Finally, it was over. All that beautiful life just left him; fell away. Nicodemus and Joseph took him down. Mary refused to let go of him for such a long time. They argued as gently as they could, and we held her back as they carried him away.

I needed to be alone this morning. I knew the stone would be heavy, but I wouldn't need much of a gap to squeeze in and light the lamp. Yet I was already too late! They couldn't even let him have his peace in death. I had run to tell the others and followed them as they came to see for themselves.

Simon stared at me as they returned to the city, shaking his head in as much shock and bewilderment as I felt.

I found myself alone again. The tears wouldn't stop now. All the horror and the pain, all that rage, all that loss. The strength I had pretended deserted me then. That was when I felt them before I saw them; felt the light. They terrified me but spoke so gently that I answered them. I said the body was lost. I said I didn't know what to do.

A twig snapped behind me. A man was there, a stranger. This early in the morning, I guessed he had to be the gardener. A tiny glimmer of hope began in me. What if the tomb hadn't been robbed after all? What if the Romans hadn't come in the night to commit some final desecration? What if the authorities hadn't seen to it that he vanished into the wilderness so that no one could ever make of his tomb a proper memorial? What if it was something much more simple? Perhaps, in their haste and despair, Nicodemus and Joseph had used the wrong grave? Maybe the gardener had moved the body to the proper place? And I could find him again and tend to him. I could give to Jesus the only thing I had left to give him. I could smooth those broken hands, anoint him properly. Say goodbye.

So, I asked him.

And we were back to where it all began for us. I was back in that moment when a man I didn't know knew me. "Mary." That familiar voice. The same smile.

I didn't know what to do. It was too much and too fast. He was there! Not a spirit. Not a fantasy my broken mind was conjuring. I could see the scars. I could smell him. He was as real as that day he first spoke my name to me. I wanted to touch him, hold on to him, but he stepped back and told me no. He was here but something was changing, and the old friendship was shifting even then. I had to learn a different kind of love.

We sat there, as the sun came up and the birds sang. And he told me what to do. Then he got up, promised me I would see him again, and walked away. I've sat here for who knows how long. The ointment is laughing at me. The whole world is laughing. And I am laughing too. To go from death to joy in a heartbeat . . .

He has just saved me all over again.

Cleopas on the Road to Emmaus

BENJAMIN AND I KNEW the road from Jerusalem to Emmaus. The inn was a regular stop for us as we traveled between the city and our homes in Lydda. These first seven miles took us upward with the hills on the Roman road before we dropped into the valley, crossed the river and climbed again to reach the village. Hannah and Andrew knew we were coming and always had a room and a meal waiting and a good fire burning.

We set off in the afternoon on that first day after the Sabbath. Passover had destroyed us and we wanted to leave Jerusalem behind. We walked away from the horror. We wanted to put distance between us. The night had closed around us; the depth of betrayal and the poison of injustice. Jesus had spoken of his end, but we had still not seen it coming until the gates closed behind him and the guards took up their places. We scrambled for news and put together what pieces we could find; a trial before the council, an early morning appearance before Pilate. There was talk of Herod questioning him as well. But whatever process there was, whatever chance there was, evaporated with the morning's mist.

I saw him taken to Golgotha. It crucified me to watch, but it was a debt I had to honor. A few of us stayed through to the very end. We heard the hammers and the screams, bones split. We watched the soldiers divide his clothes and play their dice beneath his feet. We heard him speak, such words! One dying with him, held and shamed alongside him, found it in himself to say a word of kindness. Jesus promised him Paradise!

We saw the sun refuse to shine. We watched him die.

Joseph and some of the others took his body down. They knew a tomb that he could have. We all went our different ways; staying where we had found lodgings or gathered with a few of his closest. The Sabbath passed. Ben and I got ready for the journey back. We had new leather for the workshops at home, as we always did after visiting the city. But we didn't care for business any more. What we really were packing up were the hopes of generations for our people, hopes of freedom and forgiveness, an end to suffering and loss. We had believed in the Messiah and thought we knew him. We had trusted in redemption and thought it near. We were wrong.

As we were leaving, James and John found us with news of the tomb being empty. Mary and some of the other women had gone to finish what needed to be done only to find his body gone. They had had a vision of angels who promised that he had risen from the dead! We wondered if we should stay longer. But as the morning wore on and as we talked it through, we chose to escape this place that kept on tormenting us. Of course we wanted him alive, of course we did. But what we heard seemed more to be the denial of reality than the truth. Which saw us on the road.

We were several miles out when Jesus joined us. But you have to understand that we did not know him then. He was just another traveler on the road, heading the same way we were. Nothing about him was familiar. We exchanged a few words of greeting and assumed he would walk on ahead of us. He wasn't laden in the way we were. But he didn't pass us by. He fell into step and took one of the packs from me, offering to help carry things for a bit. And then he asked us why we seemed so sad.

We stopped. Ben looked back toward Jerusalem as I summed things up. I didn't know how anyone could be coming from the city, leaving after those past few days, and have no idea of what had been happening. Roman executions weren't uncommon, but not so frequent that they went unnoticed. And the furore surrounding Jesus had got most people talking. I watched his face as I named Jesus, wondering if I might see a clue as to whether or not he was for or against us. In the circumstances it was risky. But there it was.

His retort about our slowness and our foolishness made us both bristle. Who was he to talk to us like that? Who was this stranger to take our grief and despair and treat them as next to nothing? Who did he think he was?

As our anger burned and our words sharpened, he stood his ground. And then he spoke words that stopped us: "Let me show you how the Scriptures have come true."

And that's how he began to unfold the scrolls in our imaginations. Book after book, text by text, he wove a journey that carried us from the creation of the world through the calling of Abraham and Sarah, onward into slavery in Egypt and the rise of kings in the holy city behind us. He took us to the places where people saw the work of God and walked with us beside those who had been filled with God's Spirit. With the prophets he gave us guides and witnesses who kept the hope of God's day alive even when exile and destruction seemed to end all things. He dwelt long in the Psalms with their honesty and their trust in spite of pain. In Isaiah, he opened up for us the visions of salvation that find their destiny in a suffering servant of the Lord.

The walking and the miles passed as he wove his threads and let the Scriptures tell their story. We knew the script. But we had never heard it performed like this, never seen it as the plan of God urging its way toward the life we had just lost. This stranger wanted us to believe that even the cross we saw Jesus die upon, even his tomb that lay empty, were intended; had purpose and meaning.

We reached Emmaus. The day was closing and the night was near. The stranger was going further. But we were now hungry for much more than the meal awaiting us. We invited him to stay, to talk on, to eat and rest with us. We were sure that Hannah and Andrew would find a space for him.

Later, we sat together at the table and shared good food. Just his conversation seemed to lift our spirits. We had endless questions and he let us ask them, unhurried in his replies. His knowledge of Scripture seemed boundless. And then came the moment when he took up the bread, said the blessing, broke it and shared it.

Jesus!

And he was gone!

We left at once, grabbing our things, mumbling apologies, paying the bill and practically running out the door. Hannah's confusion mingled with our own. No, not confusion. Amazement! By the time we got back to the others we had calmed down enough to tell our story simply.

The door was locked, and the friends were as eager to tell us their experiences as we were to speak of ours. And that's when he was there again, standing in the room, a ruined hand reaching for the bread.

Bartholomew, after the Ascension

NONE OF US WANTED it to end. Why would you wish for the miracle to cease when the miracle kept walking into your house? How could we ever imagine that this time would end and we would be left without him? Those days after he rose from the dead were the most precious of all because they weren't possible. The years of our traveling had been packed with enough signs and surprises to satisfy anyone. Of course they had! But these final weeks in Jerusalem have held a very special richness.

A big part of it was his forgiveness.

Our guilt and shame hung heavy round our necks. A few had not deserted him. The Marys and others, his mother, they had risked being seen to be at his side even as the soldiers took him away. They kept most of their anger hidden, but those of us who had made ourselves invisible could imagine it. I had thought myself stronger than I turned out to be when it mattered most.

I was one of the first to follow him. He found me not long after my baptism by John. It made so much sense, then, to join him as he continued what John had begun. Pretty soon, as he began to reveal himself, we could see that the things John pointed to were coming true. We could all feel the hand of God. I knew I was in the right place. Even his warnings and his challenges couldn't put me off. Others fell away, turned their backs on him, found the words too hard and the way too difficult. But I stayed and I was sure of my faithfulness.

All that changed when we got here. The city felt frightening, and we suddenly seemed so tiny; insects trapped in the web. The final days were overwhelmed with threat. He took the Passover to a new place and we didn't want to go there with him. We protested. We struggled to understand what he meant. And when we finally understood, we lost him. And I lost myself.

Gethsemane is a beautiful garden. I've always loved the stillness of the ancient olives, the moonlight or the sunshine crafting shadows around their twisted wood, the flowers, the glimpses of the city across the valley. I've always found its peace a gift so close to the press and noise of Jerusalem. But not that night. Gethsemane grew into a nightmare of soldiers and swords and betrayal. We fled. With the others, I hid, terrified that we would be found. And in the silence of those hours, as they became days, my failure ate away inside and my despair grew.

I think we all needed to hear his word of peace every bit as much as we needed to hear him call our names. When he first started to come to us, how we fumbled with our feelings! Everything collided! All that pain and loss, all those accusations, all the doubts, the disbelief and the fear and the flicker of hope. So much shifting so fast. But he knew that. For each and every one of us, he knew the things to say and the ways in which we needed to hear them said. He let us be sorry. Didn't brush away our feelings but let them roll and led us into honesty with ourselves and with each other and, most of all, with him. And that was how we began to learn what his dying truly meant. And how forgiveness sets you free.

Slowly, making the connections for us, Jesus retraced our steps together. He started to draw together the threads of things that had happened and the ways in which he had spoken of them. He reached far back into the Scriptures and the stories of our people to show how he, like John with his baptism, brought to fulfillment a host of hopes and expectations. With Jesus, events were never accidents. Now, he showed us how they lined up, creating this glorious chain of salvation as God worked to prepare the way for all that had just happened. Where we saw Jesus as the victim of others and the victim of our own failure, he showed himself to be working to God's will. He had always been showing anyone willing to notice the way to enter into the home God always had ready for us, into that place where we can know all our sins forgiven, all our brokenness restored, all our shame washed away. That's what his miracles had shown. That's what he had told in his stories. That's why he dwelt upon the texts he taught and highlighted what they offered of the ways of God amongst us.

He had taught us, as we prayed, to seek the coming of God's kingdom. Now, in the last place anyone would go looking for heaven on earth, he showed us its dawn. When he stretched his arms upon that cross, when he felt the insults come and the friends run, he was saving us all. Even our fears that God might come or care, even our despair that God might disappear, had become his journey too. He took us to the Psalm he had clung to at the end, that place of godforsakenness and grief. And now, we saw, he had carried this into the heart of the God whose son he is so that all its power to destroy us might be destroyed. Even death died on Golgotha that day. His visiting us now, his laughter and his talking, the food we shared once more, his touch, all these spoke of resurrection. And they were not just for him. They were for us all. He was tasting first the possibilities for all of us.

But this treasured time had to end. He warned us that it would. He needed to go home so that we could become everything he knew that we could be. There had been rain, and the familiar path was muddy as we climbed the hill toward Bethany. I remember we stopped and turned to take in the view of the city. Jesus drew us close. Pointing to the Temple, he told us to wait until God showed us the time had come for us to act. We were to become the next chapter, his witnesses in a world aching for words of hope and signs of God. We wouldn't have the courage or the strength on our own. We knew that all too well! But Jesus promised we would have a helper. And when the Spirit of God came, we would find it in ourselves to leave our hiding places and our silence. Starting in the city that had seen him die and seen him rise, we would tell of the things we knew. "Go everywhere," he said.

He walked on a little with us then. We asked him what else we needed to know, and he smiled and told us we had all we needed already. We hardly noticed that the mist was gathering. And then he was gone.

We stood there, staring. I was wondering if this was just another one of his recent disappearances. Was he going to be back in Jerusalem waiting for our return? "I think that's it," Thomas suddenly said. "I don't think we'll see him again now." Even as he said it, I think we all knew he was right. Here we were, on the Mount of Olives, watching the sky and feeling, all over again, how few we were, how frail. But this time we did not feel alone. This time we did not feel the shame. This time was different. He had gone, but we were not deserted or defeated.

We were waiting, and that's a very different thing.

7

Pentecost

Mary, the Mother of Jesus

JERUSALEM CALLED TO US once more. The days had slowly passed since we had held each other on Golgotha and watched. Life sucked out of us as it was ripped from him. My son!

His brothers and sisters and friends had gathered me, dragged me, tried to mend me. Then, the impossible. Word came from others at first; gossip and rumors, stories and mysteries. He was here again, walking and teaching, eating and laughing, weeping and dancing. After all we had been through together, all I had seen, all I knew, I didn't need to be convinced. I was there some of the times when he stepped back into the room. I held him in my arms the way I always had. And I let him go the way I knew I had to. He was with us in more ways than any of us could understand. Time and place could no longer hold him. And we were changing as he opened up the truths we groped toward and dimly saw.

Forty or more days had passed when we were all together in another room in the city. We often locked the doors. We knew nothing would keep him out, and we also knew that many in the city suspected us. His friends remembered that night when the soldiers had come to find them in the garden. Fear was living with us as much as hope. The world was unpredictable. Life was tumbling, racing, stumbling.

It was morning, I remember.

The sounds of the city were suddenly joined by something else. It sounded like a wind that moves the branches of the trees and begins to make the leaves rattle. It was soft and distant, just enough to notice. I could see the washing on the roof across from us. It was strange. As the girl hung each piece it dripped and held completely still as if no wind at all was there to make it move. The sound grew, swelling. Now it was like a storm approaching across the desert that blinds you with the sand or a gale that boils on Galilee and turns the water into foam. The washing on the line hung still, but the sound was roaring in our ears. The girl on the roof fled for the stairs, her hands protecting her head. Terror came. It seemed impossible that our house could stand. We clung to one another. Would Jesus come to save us? Why had he never warned us that this was how the world ends?

Then came the light.

The sun was risen but our room was brighter. I saw a net of light begin to grow against the ceiling. Yet there was no smoke and no smell of wood beginning to burn. No pop of timbers catching fire, no heat. Above our heads the light was weaving and alive. And then, like someone pouring water from a jug, the light began to fall. It flowed down and all around until everyone was caught, even those hiding under the tables.

There was no pain. No burning. And then there was nothing.

As quickly as it had come, the light vanished. And the sound had stopped as well. The street below began to stir. Voices calling and wondering. People asking questions. A baby screaming. A crowd beginning to gather. Someone shouting for order. The girl on the roof reappeared, looking around and up at the sky and then staring into the room where we were.

Where were we?

Something was new, but we could barely name it. It felt like laughter, or a taste of something sweet, or the greeting of a long-lost friend, or resting when you feel completely safe after a dangerous journey. It was embrace and longing. It was love exploding and fear overwhelmed. It silenced each one of us at first. We were all trying to understand and catch up with what we felt. Our minds were slower than our hearts. We didn't have the words to name it, couldn't find the way to speak it. We were still. Some were weeping. Some trembled. Some rocked with their eyes shut and others reached a hand to hold their neighbor.

I don't know who began to laugh, but the laughter was infectious. And words began to tumble; praise and thanksgiving, shouts of sheer joy, the sighs of someone who has endured so much, recitation from the Scriptures, holy words set dancing on the lips, prayers carried on a breathless rush of longing. We were like sleepers finally awakening, weary travelers finally finding lodging, storm-battered sailors finding a haven and the stillness of safe waters.

We still could not say what was happening to us. But we all knew that this was good. This was something sent from God. A few began to speak of teaching they remembered. Jesus had spoken of this. He had promised it. A helper would come. The Spirit of the Almighty would make a home amongst his friends. As in the ancient days when God gifted some to lead and teach and prophesize, so now amongst our frightened company. Not just upon a chosen few, but upon us all, claiming and calming us from within. So often my son had trusted in a power we did not know. Now, that same power was beginning to work in us. And then we discovered why.

The sound of knocking drew us back to reality; people were hammering at the door and shouting. Jerusalem was alive to strange events. Jesus had brought strangeness with him. Peter and some of the others were the first to move. They went out and soon we found ourselves at the center of a growing crowd. Some were simply curious. Some were laughing at us, imagining a drunken party as one more bit of our oddity. Some looked angry. Some had already started to whisper. I saw soldiers and rabbis. It was strange; here I was in Jerusalem surrounded by a crowd again. But, this time, I felt no fear.

There were many voices, many tongues, but then people started to fall silent as they listened. Jerusalem is always a magnet at festival time. People come from many places. You hear so many languages. People make themselves understood as best they can. Signing often serves. But this was different. Languages we never knew came as if we had spoken them all of our lives. You could see the shock on the faces, the amazement.

My son was doing much more than coming back to life.

A Pilgrim in Jerusalem

DEAREST FAMILY,

I hope this letter will get to you long before I can come home. I have found a trustworthy merchant who is setting out today for Cyprus. He has friends in Paphos who regularly sail to Attalia. They will deliver my words and you must offer them the very best of hospitality Pamphylia can offer when they do. They carry a strange treasure. I do not yet know all that it might mean. It is a kind of inheritance; a promise and a gift. It is not what I came to Jerusalem to find. I think, perhaps, that it has found me.

I must explain. You will think that I write in riddles. Forgive me. This is so new.

Let me begin with my arrival in the city some days ago. The journey was as long and as tiring as it usually is. As you know, the crossing to Cyprus and then on to Sidon was blessed with fine weather, calm seas and fair winds. We made good time. But then came the part I always loathe; that four-day trek with the camels along the coast road and then winding our way inland from Caesarea toward Samaria and endlessly upward through Shiloh and Bethel. There is scant shade. The pace always slows and the days pass in a fog of flies and sweat and stench. At least, this time, we didn't have to negotiate with bandits and we didn't suffer the losses of last year.

Reaching Jerusalem is always, though, a glory! The city gleamed as it always does and the traffic grew heavy on the road as we got to the gates. I was thankful that Abraham and his men were waiting for us and helped us navigate through the masses arriving for Pentecost so that we could unload in peace.

As usual, I took the first opportunity I had to visit the Temple courts and change my money before washing and making myself ready for worship. The Hulda gates were packed with pilgrims. We had to be patient as we made our way through the tunnel and up into the sunlight. Always, no matter how often, I have to stop and marvel at the glory of it. The gold and bronze of the Temple shines as if burning from within. The marble gleams as if the snows of the mountains have been sliced and fashioned into its walls. The songs of the Levites and the sounds of the crowds fill the air. I made my sevenfold journey around the Temple, dwelling deeply upon my thankfulness for the blessings of a safe arrival and praying for all of you at home. I bought the sacrifices and made my thank offering.

It was then, settling in with others in the portico, that I began to listen to the news. And what news there was! The city was alive with it! People were still speaking of an execution that had happened nearly seven weeks before. A rabbi from Galilee had embraced the cross the way too many have. It was not the first execution and will not be the last. The Romans enjoy their "reminders" and we have endured the humiliations many times. I have walked the roads when crucifixions have marked the miles, the birds pecking as we avert our eyes and hurry. He had claimed, as others have, to be the Messiah. He had generated fervent crowds and people spoke of miracles. God was with him, so it seemed. But his words brought him trouble. He became too visible, too outrageous, and too bold. People knew little of how it all unfolded, but Passover saw him hanging.

Then, the talk became strange and unsettling. Different stories. Word of him rising from the dead! People had heard it from different witnesses. His closest followers had come out of hiding and were worshipping in the Temple and seemed united in their conviction. The risk they were taking! He had died because he had claimed too much. Now they were claiming even more!

All of this would be news enough to share with you all; the holy city and the highest hopes dancing with each other. But, my dears, there is even more!

Another day came, bright and clear with the crowds at worship and the crowds in the market and the city buzzing. I was purchasing new pottery to bring home. Suddenly, the wind was tearing through the street! It came from nowhere. Except, it was not the wind. There was the sound of its fury, but nothing moved. I felt nothing. The dust did not stir at my feet. We all stared around us, craning to look up the walls of the street to see the sky. What kind of storm was this to submerge us in its sounds but not to touch a thing?

Nervous now, people got back to work. Until a new sound reached us from further down the street. This one we recognized, the sound of an excited crowd. It lured me away from my bargaining. There was a house with a step by its door. A group of men and women were standing there, gesturing, almost dancing. Around them people were pressing, trying to hear what was going on. I found myself quickly hemmed in. That's when I finally started to listen.

I will always wonder why it took me so long to notice what was happening. I think, when you have grown accustomed to speaking a different language because you have to, it maybe takes a while for the mind to understand when you no longer have to translate. They were speaking Aramaic, but not just in the Judean dialect it seemed. I was standing beside a woman who said afterward that she had come from far northeastern Galilee. She heard her familiar tongue. I thought I heard the Greek of home, such a familiar sound to my ears. Others claimed they were listening in Latin. Some were convinced they heard Parthian. Some told me later that it was all in Median and one man I met could speak only a little Aramaic and yet had understood it all. And he spoke Elamite!

Here we were, a mass of confused people and a mess of languages. Some simply denied it and mocked us all, suggesting that the wine must have been opened early! But more of us who listened were finding a word spoken directly to each one of us. It was as if, amidst the crowd, we were party to a private conversation. Out of chaos something clear was running. Think of how that thread of gold weaves its way in and out of the patterns in the tapestry in our hall. You can always follow the gold with your eyes, in spite of all the other colors that jostle to be seen.

I could hear as if I was the only person there!

And this is what I heard. I heard that the Spirit of God had come upon his friends. I heard that the prophecies had been fulfilled in this Jesus. I heard that he had come from Nazareth and had worked wonders. God had raised him three days after he died upon his cross. He is the Messiah, the Lord, the one God sends to save.

It was a word that left us all stunned. Some laughed and walked away, shaking their heads, getting on with things. Others lingered, huddled in conversation. I, along with many, drew closer. Something of this word rang true for me. It was an answer to a longing. There was a rightness to it. I felt it as much as I heard it. We asked what we should do. They told us that even now we needed to repent. And they spoke of baptism.

All of this was only yesterday. As I write, I am wondering about the way ahead for me. There is a joy inside and a longing to know more. They are meeting again this afternoon and have bid anyone who wishes to listen to them further. I will go. I must.

By the time you receive this letter, I will have found out the truth of these things. But I wanted you to know them so that, when I return, we do not need to begin at the beginning.

Do not be afraid for me. God is in this, somehow. I am sure of it!

I hold you all in my heart and in my prayers. Hold me in yours.

The Daughter of New Disciples

SOME OF MY FRIENDS want to know more about what has happened to our family. Sarah and Miriam and Ruth have been pestering me. They know we're tied up in it. Jerusalem is buzzing with it all and mum and dad haven't been keeping things exactly secret. Our stall has become a bit of a meeting place.

It's three weeks now since our world went upside down. We've been given such a lot of joy. I want to talk about it, tell the world! It's dangerous but there's so much to share. I know their angry words and the way many people look at me now. I've been pushed and "accidentally" bumped into in the street. And the stall has lost plenty of our oldest customers who don't want to be seen anywhere near us. The Temple can be difficult. We tend to stick together and try not to upset too many people. Peter and the others help us with the stories about Jesus and a bigger crowd usually starts to gather. The guards move everyone on if there are too many. But even some of them seem interested enough to linger within hearing.

It was our usual crazy Passover. Dad made sure the stall was well stocked with linens. Mum and I wound the blue threads onto their different rods ready for the weavers. We had some fine embroidery that had come in from Gibeah and there were woolens ready to be dyed. The pilgrims often want to take something home and our stall is on a good corner where many tend to linger. We had Roman customers sometimes, stocking up on something local.

I recognized Jesus when he came past. He had been in the city plenty of times and his fame meant people pointed him out. It wasn't strange to have a teacher and his disciples wandering around. But the Romans and others seemed to be taking more than normal interest in him. As the days passed things seemed to grow harder. More soldiers came. There were stories. We heard what happened later. Pilate had sent him to Golgotha and his followers were in hiding. Right then, it seemed to be just another hopeless holy man getting caught up in the politics and made into a warning. The Romans always make sure that we know where we stand.

But how are you meant to make sense of the next bit of the story? Rumors began flying around that Jesus had come back to life. That would have just been craziness if it wasn't for how his friends were acting. Instead of getting out of Jerusalem as fast as they could as we all expected when Jesus died, they stayed. Joanna, one of them, got chatting when she came to buy. She said she hadn't seen him yet, but others had. He seemed to come and go without warning. She said they knew he was as real as they were. He let them see his wounds. They were eating with him. Mum and dad weren't entirely sure how to handle it. It made me wonder.

The days went on and we were preparing to celebrate the end of the barley harvest. The city got busier again and we were kept on our toes making sure folk could get what they wanted. I was on the stall with mum. Dad was collecting more bundles of cloth. The storm came then, a mighty wind that we could hear as it tore around the rooftops. We grabbed stones to weigh things down. But, despite the noise, nothing stirred, nothing moved. It was just noise. And it left us all staring at the sky and shaking our heads.

When he finally came back, dad had more than just more cloth. He told us about the crowd he had found blocking his way. Some of the friends of Jesus were preaching. They said that the prophecies were coming true and that he had been raised from the dead. They said that he was the Messiah, God's chosen one, and that by coming back to life he was starting God's new world. And everyone could be forgiven of everything if they believed in him. Dad said they were calling anyone within earshot to join them.

Others, as they passed or as they stopped to buy, were talking about it too. We hadn't realized that we were so close to the house the friends of Jesus were using. When we closed up for the night and were back home to eat, the talk was all about what dad had heard. Could it really be true? Mum wanted to learn more there and then, I think. Dad was more cautious. He reminded us that the man at the heart of this had died on a cross, accused of defying the Romans and leading people away from God. He knew that his followers were treading a fine line. He knew we had an awful lot to lose.

And me?

I kept thinking of the look on Joanna's face as she had spoken of the strange things happening. I was remembering how she had talked about being afraid. But she had also told me of the joy; that sense of rightness to it all that meant his dying was part of something bigger, something good. What if that bigger thing was happening right now, just down our street?

The more we talked, the more we turned to the prophecies. They spoke of hopes and dreams, of God doing things that changed the world. We believed. Our whole lives, we have believed. And we have trusted in God's power and goodness even when it seemed so hidden that it might as well have vanished altogether. What was the point of prophecies if they never came true? Why hold on to hope if you don't trust it ever to turn into reality? Why do we always pray for a better day if we don't think it will ever begin?

The next day, mum and dad left me to look after the stall and went to where the friends of Jesus were. Another crowd had already gathered. Peter was there, and some of the others. They spoke again, the same message. When they came back, dad and mum both wanted to know more. And that's how our world began to begin. Over the coming weeks, we spent time listening and asking our questions. We heard about the life that Jesus had lived and the things he had done and the ways he had helped and healed. We heard what he taught. We met others who had met him. And we prayed. We prayed that it might be true and that, if it was, God would show us.

Joanna would stop and talk a lot with me. She understood my uncertainties and never laughed away my questions. She listened. And she simply told me the story of the life she had before and the life she had now.

Eventually, I asked her what I should do.

"Trust him," she answered. "Trust him with your life. Believe he can give you forgiveness. Let him fill you with the love and the hope that is his gift. Let him bring you home."

That night, I did.

Peter

I DIDN'T WANT TO leave, but Jerusalem is killing us. It makes no sense to linger. I know that. But it still feels like desertion and a failure. This is the first time I have returned to Bethany since last we came through here with Jesus. If I had known then all the things we'd see, I wonder if I would have had the stomach for it?

You knew it all of course. You always did. Right from that moment when the waves were lapping at the boat and the nets were drying on the sand, you knew how this would go. And you saw in me the person I could be long, long before I had any idea. All those miles we walked together, you talked and chided me into trusting more. I loved your stories and I loved you for the way you made them real every day. You even knew that I would fail you. And yet you stuck with me.

That night will never leave me; the end beginning. You washed my feet, carefully wiped away the dust and stain of travel. You gave us that to remember you by so that serving others would be our vocation just as it is yours. You added in the meal, the bread and wine to remember you. I remember how you sent Judas on his way and we walked to Gethsemane with you. And then, despite all you asked, I slept! I slept! Your ordeal was already under way as I lay swaddled beneath an olive tree!

Worse. When I tried to stop them you held me back, said things had to be this way. So, I followed at a distance and bluffed my way into the courtyard where the fires were lit and the guards were watchful. Three times they knew me. Three times I denied you. It was all just as you had said it would be.

I could not stay with you. Others managed it, I don't know how. The women had a strength in loving you whilst I was whimpering. They told me about your mother's courage. I hid myself away, far enough away not to hear the sounds. On the horizon, I saw three crosses rising. I watched as the sky darkened and the world became silent. I watched and wept and tore my clothes. I thought of killing myself.

But, even then, you would not let me go. Enough in me could remember your words, and your predictions that this would be the way of things. "Hold on," your silence kept on saying.

Eventually, I made my way back to the others. The shock and fear that gripped us all made them less accusing, I think. The shame in me kept me quiet. We were numbed by all of it. Someone said a prayer which trailed away into weeping. That Sabbath is a mystery to me. Thank God it finally ended.

Joseph told us where he had laid you to rest. As soon as they could, Mary and the others went to look after you properly. They'd only been gone a short time when they were back, shouting about the grave being robbed. I ran to see and found it as they said. I trailed back into the city, taking my time, walking mindlessly through the streets as life went on as normal all around me.

By the time I got back to the house the wild story was already running. Mary and others were speaking of seeing you once more, of wounded hands and feet and words of comfort and assurance. Cleopas and Benjamin arrived after their round trip to Emmaus to stun us even more with what had happened to them. And then, here you were.

It really was you. You had to take it slowly, with your peace and your touch, with the food you ate and the lengthy time you gave for all our questions. You had to be so patient with us. We knew you worked miracles. I just don't think any of us expected you to become one. And I think you enjoyed your new ability to come and go as you did. Those forty days will always be the precious memories that we treasure.

But you also made sure we didn't get too used to having you back. You were preparing us. I can see it now. You knew we were at the hinge of history, the moment when the race gets handed on to those who have been prepared to run it. The thing was that we didn't really know how. You seemed to have a lot more confidence in us than we had in ourselves. We knew that you had begun something tremendous, a new heaven and a new earth. We understood enough to know the message we were to share. We had waited long enough for the Messiah to have a pretty good idea of the script. We had all seen lives changed as people put their trust in you. We were living proof! But how might we manage to convince anyone to put their trust in you, when all you had left was us and our example? It seemed an awfully fragile way to change the world.

We lost you in the end as heaven took you home. The visits stopped and we were told to wait. You know I'm not great at waiting! And then came the festival and the power of God pouring into us, giving us a confidence we hadn't known before. I was no longer the one in hiding, but the one with things to say and share and do. I was speaking, as we all were, about who you were and what you had done. We told anyone who would listen. We found strangers from all over the place listening. We knew the risks, but the risks no longer silenced us. Our three years with you gave us so much to share and the Spirit of the Almighty gave us the courage we needed. We couldn't answer every question, did not have all the tools we might have needed. But what we had seemed to be enough because what we had were our own stories as much as your story. Each of us could speak of a life changed, of forgiveness within that gave a freedom to love the world and work for God in the heart of things. We worshipped in the Temple and we prayed together. We even found that the miracles could happen as we called upon your name.

And people joined us! Thousands of them! It was as if there was a hunger in the world and we had found the bread. How often, in those early weeks, we remembered the promises you had made: bread of life; living water; a good shepherd; the way and the truth and the life. Your language became more and more our own. We were not simply repeating it as if a lesson learned to be trotted out as necessary. It was something far more true and honest than that. Your words had become the ground we were building our own lives upon. I really did begin to understand the rock you said we needed.

We made sure the fine words also changed the way life could be. We shared. I remember those hillsides when the crowds ate their fill and we copied you in that, ensuring everyone had what they needed and holding our possessions and money in common. We wanted to be known to be a community of kindness.

It was inevitable that the backlash would come. You had died for all of this. Now we started to feel the heat. John and I were arrested twice and had to make our case before the council. Here I was, the fisherman from Galilee, talking faith and doctrine with Annas and Caiaphas and all the rest! The flogging that they gave us was agony. But it didn't stop us. Then came Stephen's death, and we knew we could not stay. He was our first martyr. We guessed he would not be the last.

Which has me here, in Bethany. I'll go home first, catch up. And then, ahead lies a future I cannot imagine. We are splitting up, travelers now, heading out from Jerusalem just as you told us to. We're pilgrims in search of destinations. I do not clearly see the way. But that no longer frightens me. It is enough that your promises come true. You live. And, by your Spirit, you live in me and in all of us. This is enough. And it is everything you promised.

8

Following Jesus on the Way

A Woman Healed of Her Bleeding

AFTER THE SYNAGOGUE PRAYERS, I often come to this square and sit in the shade. I love watching the village passing by. People stop and say hello. We talk about how their children are doing and the things that matter. Sometimes, it falls quiet, and I can be there on my own. It's different now, to how it used to be. Now, I can be happy on my own because I know it isn't a punishment. It's just that the place has grown quiet and I can safely treasure the stillness of the day. I can hear the breeze blow the dust and the leaves. I can let the sun warm me and not want to hide from the day and the eyes of others. I can be comfortable and at peace just as me. I love how normal everything is.

Normal used to mean something else for me, and for the village. Being alone was far more than a choice I was making. It was an act of faith for all of us. The distance folk used to keep, the care they took not to get too close, the care I took to stay out of other peoples' way, were what we knew. All of us were honoring God the best we could. We understood the law, and the law was God's gift. I didn't need Jairus or anyone else at the synagogue to remind me. Believe me, I have those words carved inside me: a woman who's bleeding is unclean as long as she bleeds. What she touches becomes unclean with her. And anyone who touches what she has touched becomes unclean too, until they wash and the sun sets.

We take care when the time comes for us each month. We learn this young. We expect it and we understand it and, most of the time, our periods just come and go and life continues.

But not for me.

When the bleeding started, I did the normal things, took care and waited for it to cease. When it continued, I think I went and got some help from Susanna first. As one of the oldest and wisest in the village, she suggested some remedies and offered comforting words. And that's how my suffering and punishment began; softly, gently, with kind words and little hints of hope.

The weeks gathered and then it was months, and I was washing and praying and panicking. It didn't stay my secret. Even if I was imagining it, I assumed people could smell the blood on me. No herbs or spice could hide it. Endless washing. Fresh clothes soiled and taunting me by noon. Of course, I had spoken with Jairus and the others and they had been sympathy and kindness. But they also knew the law. And the synagogue became off limits. People noticed where I went. By mutual, silent, agreement, I avoided sitting down in public. Little by little, my world was shrinking, turning into a lonely struggle that no one else could enter. People were kind, many times and in so many ways. But their kindness couldn't heal me.

The first doctor I went to forced me to let him see. I came away feeling more humiliated and unclean than ever. Many more followed, eating up my money and promising that their remedy would work. I ate all sorts of things, some of which had my stomach twisting and me on my knees in agony. I was told to sleep with my legs raised, or with my head higher than the rest of me, or only on my side. I was told not to lift anything heavy, or to exercise until I collapsed in a heap of blood and sweat. It went on and on and on. Twelve years! Twelve years of misery and shame. Twelve aching years when hope fled and friends found they couldn't keep trying. Twelve years of trying to get well, and failing. Twelve years of weakness and pain and being shut away and shut out. So much of my life stolen.

I had kept praying and believing for some of it. But God was silent. The law was clear and it was meant to be our great inheritance. But how are you meant to cope when you inherit your own personal prison? How do you keep trusting when the mighty one gives you nothing good, nothing to offer even the slightest glimmer of possibility? What was the sin that deserved this? What sin from the past generations had stuck to me? How do you pray when you are in a tunnel of pain that never ends? I know others were praying for me, hoping for me when they knew I had lost mine. I knew I was loved. But their love wasn't quite so real when I was awake in the night, on my own, changing the bed again, hating my body.

I'll never know quite how Jesus broke through to me. His reputation was growing, and I had heard some of the stories. We all had. There were miracles happening, healings and hope. Holy men came and went. But he seemed different somehow, if even some of the stories were true. With him, God seemed to be working wonders and people were finding life in ways that never seemed possible. Whatever it was, something in me wanted to trust him, wanted to believe again. Desperation maybe.

The sickness that took hold of young Amira had Jairus and Margalit consumed with worry. I felt for them and their lovely daughter. I had plenty of insight into the kind of fear that was crushing them now. The arrival of Jesus had the village running. He was soon at the center of the crowd, and it wasn't long before Jairus appeared, all dignity thrown away as he ran and pushed and screamed for help. The crowd started to move in the direction of the house where Amira lay dying. Naturally, I was the outsider, carefully keeping my distance, walking slowly to avoid bumping into anyone, hoping not to be noticed.

And then something snapped in me. Why not me? Why not help me? Why not do like Jairus and push my way to him and beg him to heal me? Why not risk polluting everyone? What if this was the only chance I had?

Almost without being aware of it, I had my head down and covered and started to edge my way into the crowd. I think the excitement of having Jesus here and the drama of the moment made folk ignore me. I was pushing and edging my way and everyone I touched was being made unclean. But no one was noticing. No one was caring. No one scolded me.

But my courage started to seep away the closer I got to Jesus. Maybe I didn't need to actually speak to him at all. Maybe, if I just touched his cloak? Maybe the unclean in me would meet the holy in him and something could happen. And, if it didn't happen, I could slip away unnoticed and deal with the shame and anger one more time. And so, head down and hand reaching ahead of me, I got to the middle of the crowd and found him.

"Who touched me?"

I almost bumped into you, you stopped so suddenly. Wonder was at work in me! I knew, absolutely knew, that I was healed already. I was holding my belly and raised my head to find you staring right at me. People were wondering what you were talking about. Beside you, Jairus looked frantic, tugging your arm, begging.

But this had become my time. Overwhelmed, I fell at your feet and started babbling. I didn't say much. But you heard me, truly heard me. You heard the suffering. And you saw me, truly saw me. You lifted me to my feet. And you said, loud enough for everyone to hear, that I was as much a daughter of Abraham as anyone else. You said it was my faith that had carried me here. You promised that your peace and healing would keep me safe from now on.

Even as I was trying to take it all in, someone was speaking to Jairus, and he crumpled. But your work wasn't done. You spoke of not being afraid. Turning back to me, you smiled and squeezed my shoulder, and then you were swallowed by the crowd as you moved on.

I was left standing on my own. But my loneliness, and so much more, were gone.

One of the Disciples Jesus Sends Out to Share the Good News

THERE WERE SO MANY things we didn't know when you started to send us out. Just as well. Had we seen everything we might never have gone very far. Ignorance can be a comfort.

We were heading toward Jerusalem with you when things changed. I don't remember which village it was that we were passing through when you called us all together. We made quite a sight because we were quite a crowd. We must have numbered nearly a hundred. You gathered us in a field on the side of the road and spoke about the time being right for us to play a much bigger part in your work. You invited us to find a partner and told us you were going to send us out to spread the word and share your power with the people we met. Seventy of us did so and you asked us to sit together with you as the morning drew on and the sun rose higher above the hills. There were fires lit and food was cooking already.

John and I were close to you as you started. You spoke of the world as a field ready for harvest and told us that we were to share in the harvesting. The harvest would be lives turning more and more toward the realm of God. You reminded us of how we had been before we knew you. Some of us had a very great faith. Some of us had wandered far away from the things of holiness and the praise of God. Some of us were burdened with guilt and many of us had questions that defied answers. Whilst some of us approached the world with arrogance and seemed sure of ourselves, most of us felt pretty small in the face of growing hostility and suspicion. Most of us had left someone or something behind to follow you. We had all spent our time weighing up whether or not to pitch in with your odyssey. We had met some of the opposition and been stung by it. We had watched others walk away.

You told us that you wanted us simply to spread out and wander away into the hills and along the tracks. "Don't set a destination. Just let the Spirit lead." And, as we met people, you said we needed to offer a greeting worthy of you. We were to be bringers of peace and witnesses to hope. You told us that the great power we had was the story we could tell of what we had found when you found us. "You'll have the words you need when you most need them. You'll find you have enough when you say what you have seen me do and heard me say." You told us not to be afraid to say we did not have the answer to every question or the solution to every problem.

When some asked you how long we would be away and what we need-ed to pack, you said that we must travel light and rely upon the hospitality of strangers. You wanted your ways of trusting and wandering to become our ways. You wanted us to let go of all our calculation and all our planning. "Just see where God takes you," you said.

Raising your hands in blessing, you told us that we went in your name to do the work of God. You said that your power would be our protection, and you promised to be praying for us every step we took.

John and I looked at each other. Gradually it was dawning on us all that you meant for us to make a move there and then. You were on your feet, moving among us, offering a quiet word. When our turn came, you told us to come back to this spot the day after the Sabbath. "Don't be afraid," you said as you smiled. "Salvation is here and you have tasted it already. It is God's gift. Don't hoard it. Let others know what you have found."

"Let's head south," John suggested. And so we went.

By the time we returned six days later, we had visited four villages. We had invented a way of doing things. We would settle into the public space and wait to see who might be about. We would greet everyone we met. Often, people would offer a quick word and then get on with their business. Some ignored us completely. The looks we got from others told us we were not about to find a welcome. In the first three places we gave up after a day of waiting when it felt as if no one was going to give us a hearing or any kind of hospitality. Each time, as we prepared to walk away, we stood and prayed aloud. We prayed that they might know how close the kingdom of God had come and how much they had missed.

These first three attempts depressed us. We felt ourselves to be failures and we worried at what you would say when we returned. Who needs dis-ciples who can't even share the message they've heard? We imagined the incredible success stories the others would tell . . .

But we also found ourselves remembering some of the ways folk responded to you. We might be part of a big company, but we were tiny compared to all those around who had either never heard anything about you or who had rejected you. We thought of Nazareth and how those who had watched you growing up found it hardest to let you be more than the son of Joseph and Mary. We consoled ourselves with these memories. Nothing was simple and nothing was inevitable. Everything was about choices. People had to be willing to listen and ready to understand. Trusting you wasn't obvious.

It was John who remembered your story of a man sowing seed, and how the sower had to risk plenty of seed falling on ground that would not receive it. "Maybe the thing we're learning is that the sower never knows for sure where the good soil is going to be," John wondered. "The point of being the sower is that you just have to keep on trying to get seed into soil and then wait and see what happens."

The day came when we were in another village square. As usual, we smiled and offered a word to anyone who seemed ready to give us a moment. An old man came along, exchanged a greeting, and sat beside us on the wall. We got talking. He wondered where we were from and what brought us here. We told him. He asked a question. We offered an answer. He asked another. Without us really noticing, a conversation had begun and other people started to join in. Eventually, there must have been a dozen or so of us chatting in the sunshine. Someone suddenly asked us if we were hungry. "Starving!" we answered together. An invitation was offered. A boy was sent off to warn a family.

John and I had never known such a welcome! The table was laden and the house was full of people as friends and neighbors slowly gathered to hear us tell what we had to say. Often, we had to repeat things as someone new arrived. The day slipped toward evening and we were offered beds for the night. It was glorious to sleep in a real bed after so many nights under the stars, to wash and feel clean. To find a welcome like this among strangers.

The next day, as we prepared to leave, a small crowd gathered around us. They had brought a child on a stretcher who had been ill for many days. John knelt down and placed his hand upon the girl's head. He and I prayed. We asked that, in the name of Jesus, she be made well. Everyone was quiet, watching, waiting. She opened her eyes and smiled.

"And some seed fell on good soil," John murmured, "and produced a hundred times the normal crop."

The Syrophoenician Woman's Faith

OF COURSE I WAS up for the fight! Wouldn't you be? Wouldn't you do every single thing in your power to save your child? Wouldn't you take every risk and go every mile to bring your child home? I had carried her in my womb, felt her kick me in the night. I had screamed as she came into the world, and I had held her tight and nursed her. I had counted her teeth as they came. I had watched her take her first steps and listened with delight to the words she began to speak. And I had done all of this with my husband at sea, coming home all too briefly. I had held her in my arms as we stood watching his ship return and as we waved him out of sight on the high tide. I had been the one to tell Adonia of the storm, and Hanny never coming home again. So, yes, I knew what it was to protect my baby and I knew what it meant to fight for both of us.

Possession came one night. Adonia woke me with her screams. She was sweating and churning in the sheets, her eyes open but unseeing. Her screams grew still as I lay with her and stroked her hair. I hoped that it would pass. I prayed that the morning would see her returned to me. My prayer wasn't answered. The days passed. She would get better for a while, be more like her old self, and then the fever would return and she would fade away. It was haunting horror for me; a flitting between life and a living death. I sought out all the help I could. Prayers, potions, exercises, diet, all tried, none of them making much difference. I started to imagine this might be the rest of our lives; me nursing her, Adonia existing on the edge of the world.

It was my sister who first told me about the Jew. He had arrived a few nights before, slipping quietly into Tyre after dark. He was, apparently, something of a character back home. He had a reputation, it seemed, for powerful teaching and mighty acts of power. He could heal the sick. That was all I needed by way of invitation!

Despite her protests, my sister agreed to watch over Adonia whilst I headed off for the house she had told me about. As I walked, I wondered what I might say. I knew that he could brush me aside. Jews and Gentiles often try hard to avoid each other. Certainly, a notable rabbi and holy man could easily be expected to shun a strange woman begging for help in the night. But I kept reminding myself that he was the one who had come to us. He had wandered far enough away from Galilee to enter our lands. He was staying in a house in Tyre by the mighty ocean, far from home. He was hiding amongst us. Perhaps he was hiding from others. Whatever his story was, it meant he wasn't staying safely at home. He was already out of place. And, just maybe, that meant he wasn't going to play the same old games we play to keep ourselves apart.

When I knocked, they weren't at all sure about letting me in. Clearly, this couple were friends of his and they weren't pleased that word was getting around. But they heard enough of my story, saw enough of my fear and my desperation, to open up. He was reclining at the table, a meal in front of him, half eaten. He looked up as I entered, surprise on his face.

My carefully prepared arguments fled. I fell to the floor and begged. I told him about Adonia, about the fever and the spirit that held her captive. I told him of the hard years of widowhood, of bringing up a child and watching her slipping away. I pleaded with him for help: "I hear you have the hands of a healer. Heal my child. Please, in your mercy, make her well."

He listened. It felt as if he might be willing. But then he replied: "I've come to feed the children first. It isn't fair to take their food and throw it to the dogs."

There it was. The inevitable. Here was the Jewish rabbi at his meal, interrupted by the weeping Gentile woman on her knees. Here was the ancient and cruel truth. He didn't need to help me because I was a foreigner, and he wasn't going to help me. Adonia could die for all he cared. He didn't have Gentiles to save. He had come to save the Jews and we were no more than puppy dogs to him.

I felt the man of the house move up behind me.

"Lord, even the dogs under the table get the scraps the children drop."

It was all I could think to say. It was my last chance. If my place was where the scraps fell, then let me grab any scrap I could. If Adonia's only chance was a tiny trickle of kindness from this holy man, then let me just find that. If all we had to hold on to was the chance that a bit of mercy might come our way, then let us take hold with all our might! I was not going to get off my knees until he either helped us or had me taken away. I was staring hard at him now, daring him to push me out.

The moment stretched into a silence.

I was willing him to change his mind. I didn't know what else to do. He sat back, folded his arms, returned my stare.

And then, he nodded. He opened his arms wide.

"Good answer! Go back home. Your daughter is well already."

I was breathing hard.

"Thank you," I whispered.

He was smiling now. I got to my feet. He stood as well. When I reached the door, I turned back to him. "Go in peace sister," he said.

I ran.

My sister was waiting for me. She held her finger to her lips as I rushed up. She hugged me tight. "She's safe," she said as she stroked my hair. Then, taking my hand, she led me to the bed. There was Adonia, breathing gently, her face relaxed. I knelt beside her and kissed her forehead, very softly. She stirred and her eyes opened. She grinned.

"Mamma."

The Woman Who Heard about a Lost Coin

I THINK MOST OF us have lost things. You have a precious and cherished something, and then it's gone. Some of us get forgetful. Some of us live with so much chaos that it's a wonder we hang on to what we do. You should see the mess at our place! Our place is so small and there are so many to make room for.

Sometimes, people get lost. I know what that can be like. You make some bad choices. You find yourself doing things you never thought you would do. Maybe it starts off with small lies and slight shame. But, like a cistern filling with the rain, the person you thought you were or wanted to be gets drowned. Somehow, all those choices and decisions, and some of the people you've run with, have accumulated. Somewhere, you've got lost. Your life isn't what you thought it could be and you aren't the person you want to be. Too much has gone.

Perhaps all this happens, and we don't really notice it happening. We just think life is the way it is. We assume we are all we can be. There's nothing to change. Maybe we carry on and on, living with a bit of shame and sadness but never moving on.

Bring God into the story and things get more complicated. Talk of God can add to the shame and multiply the guilt that we carry. If it is hard to forgive people for the wrongs they've done, if it's hard to say sorry to them, how much harder to do that with God. How can you say sorry to the one who is perfect? How can all our failures and disasters and hurt be felt, let alone accepted and forgiven, by the mighty creator of the stars? How do we even begin to go there?

Here's how.

We find ourselves in a small crowd, sitting on the beach at Capernaum. There are fishing boats drawn out of the water, and others bobbing in the slight breeze. Nets are being mended. Gulls are circling and screaming, hoping for scraps. There's the smell of charcoal fires and fish being smoked.

We're here because we're intrigued. Jesus is a familiar figure now. He comes and goes but he and his friends can often be seen here. This beach is a favorite spot of his. So, when I heard that he was teaching here, I wandered down. I'm not as religious as many who are here. I can see some of the leaders in a huddle over there, and they are devoted men. They learn for years, and they work hard at being true to God's ways. They hold faith dear. I know I am nowhere near them.

But people have been saying that Jesus is up to something different. He's offering a glimpse of God that seems special. I've got friends who have listened to him and come away changed. None of them have run off and turned into disciples. But some have found a peace I've never seen in them before. People have started praying as if they mean it. Mary has started talking about God is if she's able to have a chat with the angels!

I didn't come here thinking any of this might happen to me. I didn't come because I thought I needed saving. I just wondered what the fuss was and wanted to hear him for myself.

Which puts me in this crowd. And Jesus had been talking for a bit, and it was perfectly good stuff. Yet, somehow, it felt a bit far away. And then he told his two stories. That's when he had me. I never thought of myself as lost until he suggested what being lost might be. And I had never imagined that God might come looking for me.

He asked us to imagine a shepherd with the flocks. The count turns up ninety-nine. One has got lost somewhere in the wilderness. The shepherd has options. Let the one go and keep the ninety-nine safe. Or, more risky, leave the flock where they are and go hunting for the lost one. This shepherd takes the risk. He heads off, following whatever signs he can find. Maybe he's calling and whistling as he goes. He's hunting hard because the sheep that he's lost is precious to him. He can't just let it go to its doom. He can't rest until he finds it. And he does find it. Scooping it up onto his shoulders, he brings it back. And the bit of the story that really took hold of me was that Jesus stressed the rejoicing and the joy! The shepherd is singing his way home because finding the lost sheep is the best thing that could possibly happen for them both. And then Jesus said that this was the way heaven sounded when one lost soul found salvation.

Someone who didn't think they mattered to God discovered that they did, and heaven was singing! Someone who worried that their messy life couldn't be treasured by God found out that it was, and heaven was dancing! Someone who imagined they couldn't ever be truly forgiven found out that they were, and heaven wept with joy.

The idea of it caught me. I never expected it, never thought of things this way. To imagine God like this, a rescuer and a seeker, a shepherd searching just for me. Jesus had my full attention now. Could this be what it really was like to be friends with him? Could he make a story like this turn real for someone like me?

He hadn't even finished. Now we were in the home of a woman who had ten silver coins. She knew their value. It was all her wealth in the world! One is lost. Nothing else matters now but finding it. She lights a lamp to peer into the darkest corners. She lifts the rugs. She moves everything in case it has fallen behind the pots. She goes through all the blankets and clothes in case it has got caught up in them. She sweeps and searches through the dust and sand. She even pours out all the flour and spices in case it got dropped in amongst them.

Finally, she finds it! And, again, there's rejoicing! She gets her friends in and they all share in her delight and relief. Finding the lost brings infectious joy.

It's the joy that has kept me thinking. Jesus has gone on his way. I never spoke to him. I never talked with the friends he travels with. I just listened to his stories and now I can't stop wondering about them. The God he wants me to know is a celebrating God who rejoices as we turn toward him more and more. The heavens Jesus points to are singing and dancing, filled with laughter whenever someone shifts their life toward the ways of holiness. Faith, for Jesus, is less about the burdens of doing the right things and more about being found. It is not so much what I do to please God as what God does to seek me out. And Jesus wants us to know that God is seeking hard for us, looking everywhere, going deep into whatever wilderness we have put ourselves in. This God is sweeping the land to try to find me because I matter. I'm a precious coin that God cannot bear to lose. We all are!

And I've found myself dwelling upon the other part of the stories Jesus told. All this rejoicing can only begin if I let it. I have to choose to let myself be found. I have to choose to come home. I have to wake up to being lost. I have to know I need to be forgiven because that's when I can be forgiven.

Everything can be different for me. But only if I let God in. Only if I trust this Jesus and all his stories.

Do I dare?

A Sister of Jesus after the Stoning of Stephen

No, I was not surprised. By the time the news got as far as Nazareth, we already knew that opposition was growing. I had never met Stephen, but my brother James had told us about his passion and his care for some of the friends of Jesus in Jerusalem. Getting close to my big brother had always been a risky business, and the risks just kept climbing. Dying now seemed to be part of the deal. Which was terrifying as we tried to protect the children and live like a normal family.

Normal family!

No chance. We were never a normal family. We started off okay, but things spun out of control fairly early. I was the youngest. Jesus was the oldest. Then came James and Joses, Miriam, Esther, Judas, and Simon. Being the youngest of eight is enough of a challenge for most kids. Having your oldest brother turn out to be the son of the living God and the Savior of the world throws normal down the well.

Growing up we had our fun and we had our fights. Jesus was serious sometimes and there were periods when he would need to be by himself or lost in arguments with adults. But he and I were always the fastest runners, and we would race each other up the hill to see who could get to the old stone first. I think we ended up pretty even in terms of victories, even if we did sometimes let the other win just out of the goodness of our hearts or because the day was hot. And then we would sit up there on the rock with the trees and the bees and we would watch Nazareth busy about its day. We would talk about the things that mattered. Friends who were in and friends who were out, why brothers can be so annoying and why sisters can be so impossible, and why parents can be both. I pestered him about his carpentry, and he would test me on my weaving. He knew I loved to work with the loom and to try different combinations to find new ways to work a pattern. I was the "weaver of magic" he used to call me. Sometimes others would find us, but most of all I loved the days it was just the two of us and the stillness.

He started to make an impression as he got older. The leaders in our synagogue quickly found him an eager pupil and slowly discovered him to be a challenging critic. It wasn't that he wanted to upset people, at least not then. At least, I don't think so. But his questions were sharp, and his understanding was deep and some found that intimidating. Once or twice, father had people grumbling about Jesus as we came home.

Everything changed when he was baptized by John in the river. He came home and had already left us in his imagination even before he walked off toward the wilderness. Mother and father were worried and upset, but not angry. They said he had to do what he was here to do. I was married by then, heavy with our first child. I never said goodbye properly.

Later, as the final years unfolded, he would reappear. Sometimes he was on his own and he would stay and talk and play with our children like anyone else's uncle. Sometimes he had his friends with him. They would come in various combinations: fishermen and tax collectors, young people who adored him, the fairly wealthy, and the pretty penniless. Sometimes we had warning, or mother would ask if we could put one of them up for a few nights. Other times they just appeared, hoping for a meal and a rest before the dusty road beckoned to them once again. Jesus was unpredictable and loved to surprise.

With these visits, ahead of their arrival and after they had gone, came the stories. Incredible stories! Broken people being healed when no one else could help. Forgotten folk who found that Jesus knew their names before they ever set eyes on him. People who were as far from holiness as anyone could be discovering that their sins could be forgiven and that the God of heaven loved them too. Angry men and abused women having their hearts remade and their lives set free. Clever people in love with great ideas being told little tidbits about mustard seeds and yeast and coins being lost and found. Families finding love again when love was dead. The dead finding life. And the more we heard, the more we worried about where this was all going to take him and where it just might carry the rest of us. Families can enjoy a little reflected glory and they can suffer plenty of reflected suspicion.

The cataclysm gathered slowly over us. I was there when he said that Isaiah was coming true in our synagogue that Sabbath. I was pointed to when people were getting angry, when they accused Jesus of getting ideas way above his station. They knew the carpenter's son; they knew our family. They knew I was his little sister. That was a preview of how his words could do something other than teach and how his touch could do something other than heal. We sometimes tried to stop him, or at least rein him in a bit. But he could be sharp with his response as he focused all he had upon all he felt called to.

When news came of his arrest, I was playing with our children, pretending to be a queen whilst they were the soldiers of my guard. Their game continued as my tears began. That night there was no sleep. Mother and some of my brothers were in Jerusalem. We could only wait and pray and hope and worry. It takes two days to get to Nazareth. My brother was in his grave long before we heard about his crucifixion.

I couldn't stay. I needed to be there, with my mother and my brothers and my sole surviving sister. I had to be in Jerusalem. Josh understood. We had friends who took in the children and we left. We camped for the night under the trees. By the time we reached the city the week was begun. And by the time we found the others, Jesus was waiting!

I remember that he held me close as I wept and let me hold his hands where the scars pierced his wrists. We didn't know how to respond. It felt too big. Others were singing and dancing and crying with delight. I needed time alone with him. He took me for a walk one day, back into Gethsemane. We sat under the olive trees as the dusk crept in and I rested my head upon his shoulder. "I'll be leaving," he said. "This way of meeting me must end so that I can be with everyone everywhere. It will be hard again for you and mother and the rest."

To say goodbye again broke my heart. Josh and I returned to Nazareth, wondering at what might be. News slowly came as family and friends arrived home. Mother and the others had received the Spirit of God! They were no longer in hiding but were speaking about Jesus to anyone willing to listen. There was talk of healings. Peter was defending the followers before the council. The fisherman was arguing Scripture and faith with the high priest! But things were turning bad despite these wonders, or maybe because of them. Jesus had died because his way with God unsettled powerful people. Now my big brother was blessing and disturbing in equal measure as people tried to understand, as some found life and others found folly. He was changing everything because he lived.

Some friends escaping Jerusalem passed through Nazareth with stories of public denunciation and worse. And then came news of Stephen.

We are all just trying to understand what is happening. We know the world is changing, but we don't yet know all that means. God is working mighty wonders, changing lives, unpicking so much that hurt, granting forgiveness, setting hope alive. Jesus is weaving something new and beautiful. He has done so much and given so much, and yet he seems to have just got started. But I can't see all of it yet, and the work of unmaking and remaking is scary when it's your life and your children who are on the loom.

I know that Jesus is the heart of it still. I know his love and care runs deeper than any sea. But, still, I am afraid now. Everyone knows we're part of his family. There's no place to hide if we stay in Nazareth. But where else can we go? Is fear another gift my big brother has left behind?

The Ethiopian Eunuch

I HAVE NEVER SEEN Philip again. But the journey he led me into has continued. It comes with its challenges and failings; I am so often alone in my believing amidst others who worship their own gods. I have seen some in my family and at the court converted, though. My testimony is simple, the story of that visit is what I offer. And the life I have been living ever since bears its own witness. Certainly her majesty, the Queen Mother, has commented upon the change in me and we have spoken long about the Savior who found me on the road.

The Candace has always been generous in allowing me my pilgrimages, even if she doesn't follow my turn toward the faith of the Jews that has been part of my life all these years. She trusts and respects me for the care I take with her affairs and the scrupulous ways in which I deal with her tenants and traders. The palace in the heart of Meroe runs smoothly and the treasury is neither wanting nor greedy. We have been together for over twenty years, and she has relied upon me in many ways. All of us have continued to navigate our relations with the Romans, retaining what power and independence we can whilst accepting their imperial hold. For my part, I am her devoted servant and faithful subject of our King.

Jewish merchants have made the road to Kush for centuries, and we have traveled north to them with our grains and our iron and gold. My duties brought me into regular contact with them, and several have become good friends. That's how my fascination with Judaism began. Asher and Lemuel in particular have shared much of their faith with me. It was their suggestion that I finally make the trip to Jerusalem for myself. I was returning from my third pilgrimage to the Temple when I met Philip.

The Gaza road was fairly quiet for the time of year. We passed several caravans heading north and showed our credentials to the Romans guarding the forts. They were polite enough when they realized who I was. Soon we were on the open stretches, the wilderness reaching into the distance all around us. We stopped when the heat was at its worst and the men would raise the canopies to offer some welcome shade. This far from anywhere we kept sentries just in case of ambush.

It was toward the close of one of these days of endless sand and rock that I was wrestling with one of the papyrus scriptures I had brought with me to study in the Temple. The Greek was easy enough to read, but the meaning was a mystery:

> "Like a sheep he was led to the slaughter, and like a lamb silent before its shearer, so he does not open his mouth. In his humiliation justice was denied him. Who can describe his generation? For his life is taken away from the earth."[1]

There was much in this part of Isaiah that baffled me. The prophet sees a servant of the Lord who undergoes tremendous suffering. Somehow all of the pain and anguish is a work in which the ways of God unfold, even a work of salvation and redemption. But who is this servant and how can suffering save? Is he a martyr in whom the nation can discover an example? Is his death at human hands or driven by divine plan? What is this price he must pay, and for what purpose? So often the prophet sees him as a figure scorned and rejected, yet in his abandonment something glorious is begun. How can God be seen in such things so far from glory? How is the power of the angels at work where all is powerlessness and fatigue and failure?

I was reading and re-reading and confused. And then came Philip.

I didn't know who he was then. I hadn't noticed him walking beside the chariot. Nor, it seemed, had the guards who suddenly shouted a warning. Startled, I found myself looking down at a Jew whose clothes bore the dust and stain of a long journey. He seemed oblivious to the arrows aimed at him and the stamping of the horses as we stopped.

"Do you understand what you are reading?"

It wasn't a question I ever expected on the road to Gaza. Something in his manner and his question made me like him already. If this was an attack, it was superbly done. I said I could read the words but did not know their meaning. I said I lacked a guide. He offered himself. I waved the archers to put down their bows. I invited him to join me and to explain himself. The captain rode up and, seeing my approval, started trotting alongside us as we

---

1. Acts 8:32b–33

set off. His sword was in his hand and he made sure the stranger could see it, a little insurance.

Very quickly, all thoughts of danger slipped away. Our conversation was like an ocean that one sees only in the far distance at first, the merest hint of something vast and grand. The more we talked, the more that ocean came into view and I was on the shore, its waters welcoming and wonderful.

He told me he was Philip, originally from Bethsaida Julias on the farthest shores of Galilee. He had been a carpenter. But that life had passed. Now, he was a follower of what he called "The Way." And he was its messenger. More than this. Our meeting was no accident. He told me of how the Spirit of God had brought him to this place and taught him of my need. It was the hand of God that was at work upon our road.

"I want to understand the prophecies," I said.

"To understand them, let me tell you the story of the man who lived them."

He started with Isaiah. He set out the ways in which the songs speak again and again of the servant who will suffer. And then he took me with him on the journey he had made these past few years. He had been met by Jesus of Nazareth, and that had changed his life. This Jesus was his rabbi and much more. In his life and words and works of might and generosity, the blessing and judgment of God flowed. But his final great act began as he took upon himself the script Isaiah spoke of. In him the suffering servant became a man dying upon a Roman cross outside the walls of Jerusalem. Yet that was never going to be the end. It was truly just the beginning! Three days later and he was alive again!

He appeared many times to Philip and to others, proving his reality as he ate and drank with them. Death could not claim him. Philip spoke of how they had begun to understand not just the ancient prophecies but also the teaching Jesus had shared as they walked with him. His death was no interruption in his work, but the culmination of it. He was carrying away all that might separate anyone from God the Almighty; all sin, all suffering, all hatred, all shame. All was defeated and their power undone. For this Jesus was no rabbi. He was the Messiah, the chosen one, the Savior, even God's own Son!

By now, my officer had put his sword away and was listening with nearly as much awe as consumed me. Philip spoke of how the Spirit of God had been shared amongst them just as Jesus promised. This same Spirit was guiding and directing him now, easing his fears and weariness, provoking him to walk beside the chariot of an Ethiopian in the wilderness.

We came upon a pool surrounded by date palms. In the distance were tents, their fires lit. We could hear the sound of flocks. Philip had spoken of baptism. It was a tradition amongst the Jews, a sign of life being turned toward God and away from selfishness. Jesus had been baptized and so were his followers. It marked the beginning of The Way; life turned toward the life that God intended.

Why not me? Why not here? Why not now?

"Do you believe that Jesus died for you?" Philip asked as we stood up to our knees in the cool water. "I do," I said. And even though this was all so new to me, it was a commitment that seemed to have been waiting for me all along. I had come home. God reached out and welcomed me and filled my heart with joy. And ever since, I have believed.

Saul

IT WAS SAFER TO sit still than fumble around that stranger's house. I was so weary of the falling and the crash. I detested my stumbling and oblivion. That havoc I was gifted with terrified me. I neither ate nor drank. The days crawled. Judas did his best to make me welcome and keep me calm. But I could hear the family muttering in their fear. Who could blame them? My reputation rested upon my zeal. Word of me traveled ahead as my messenger; always. Now, here I was, God's own warrior, blind and gabbling in their home.

Things changed when Ananias arrived. Lord, how everything changed! You claimed me, and at last I understood why I could never crush them. I had them locked and beaten, stripped of status, cast out, declared unholy, branded as heretics. I watched them die. Few followers of Jesus had never heard my name. Their fear was my addiction, their destruction my passion. I wanted to end them all. I never understood. I was so sure I had the truth.

I will never forget holding the cloaks and tunics so the stone-throwing could have more force. Watching a man die is brutal, I know, but how I approved as the life was beaten out of Stephen. How he prayed! How I despised him then in his arrogance and fantasy. How I must live with that now.

Ananias came with Judas and explained who he was. Judas excused himself, left us together. I sat silent and still. I had heard his name in my dreams, seen this moment in my mind. As he told me of the vision that had brought him, I felt the tears in my blind eyes. He called me "brother," and I caved in. I had no passion left, no strength at all. I was trembling. He laid his hands upon me, gently stroked my face. I felt his breath. Until a few days ago I had been hunting him down. I had come to Damascus to find him and all the rest. I had come with authority to seek them out, seize them, and drag them back to Jerusalem for trial. I had come to seek and to destroy. And here he was, all gentleness despite his trembling. No words of bitterness. No accusations. No threats. No retribution. Just the softest touch and the calmest words. It was love, where love should not have been. It was God, where God need not have been.

He said he had been sent by the one I had come to attack. He invoked the name of Jesus. He called for the Spirit of God to fall upon me. And, as he did so, I could begin to see again! Light and shade and shadow and movement. And then the clearest sight. There were tears running down his face as I saw him for the first time. We stared at each other, both of us transfixed.

"It is done," Ananias said.

Yes, so much had been done and so much more undone.

It was six days ago that I set out from the capital, my mission clear. My studies at the feet of Gamaliel, my devotion as a Pharisee, focused me with total conviction upon God's call to root out the heresy of the Nazarene. With my people, I loved and honored God. I treasured the ways of faith handed down to us from generation to generation. Holy Scripture and all that it commanded shaped my life, as it shaped and held and healed us all. Zeal for the Lord filled me.

Damascus seemed a likely place. Far enough away from Jerusalem for his followers to seek it as a refuge as we routed them. Big enough and busy enough to hide in. The synagogues there would be my starting point. We knew his followers tended to stick close to our worship even as they peddled their lies and heresies.

We were well on the way, about half a day's walk from the gates. There were three in our party, me and Jacob and Malachi. It was an explosion of light. Too bright. Silent and sudden and terrifying. I knew in an instant, even as the ground took me, that my sight was gone. There was no burning, no sound of thunder, no storm. Just that awful light. Where were Jacob and Malachi? Was this death? Was the world ending?

And then came the voice. It came from everywhere. It fell from the sky and rose from the rocks. We were held within it, trapped. I curled in the dust, my hands hiding my face. I could not bear to hear my name. But my name it was that was spoken; spoken with power but not with fury.

"Who are you, Lord?" I guessed a messenger from God.

But nothing prepared me for his answer, "I am Jesus, whom you are persecuting."

Jesus!

I was staggering to my feet as I sensed my friends. My eyes were open but I was blind. They guided me to a place of shade, and we sat. They had heard his voice but seen no one. As I spoke of the light, they said they had seen no such thing. Our conversation ran out. Each of us struggling to make sense of it. Each of us trying to understand. But me, most of all, falling and falling.

If they had not heard it, I might have been able to convince myself of a delusion. Perhaps the heat of the day had snatched my senses away. Stumbling on the track, maybe I had hit my head and some delirium had spoken in my mind. But they had heard him! We had all heard the impossible. The crucified one, his body stolen, calling me by name, as if he lived and knew me. More. Wanted me. Needed me. Had work for me.

We could not stay. We feared to linger. We gathered our possessions; I took my staff in one hand whilst Malachi led me. We set off again, slowly now, me feeling my way with the stick and both of them talking me through. It seemed an age but finally I heard the city, smelt the crowds and the animals. We passed the gate and they took me to Straight Street where Jacob had a friend, Judas. They persuaded him to take me in. I had arrived. But no longer the hunter. Now I was the hunted; haunted too. My world a tumbling mess of anguish and fear.

I had come to root him out. He had come to ask me why? I had come to end the lies they told about him. He had come to let me hear the truth. I knew who I was, respected what I was and cherished all I believed in and stood for. He, knowing this, spoke to me as if I might become a friend.

None of it made sense. None of it seemed possible.

Until I found myself in the arms of Ananias, my new brother.

Cornelius

HERE'S OUR HOUSEHOLD ALTAR. Like Roman families across the empire, we gather here in the morning and in the evening to light the lamps and let the incense fill our senses with its smell and treat our eyes as the smoke curls upward. We always have fresh flowers to adorn this sacred place. It isn't much, just a shelf here in the corner, but it is in every sense the heart of our home. And it is also our rebellion. Some might even say our treachery.

This house in Ephesus has been home for five years now, ever since my retirement. Its gardens get the morning sun, and we often sit beneath the magnificent cypress to talk and to remember. The wind carries the salt from the sea, and we watch the ships in the distance as they head westward toward Athens and Corinth or set sale for the long run to Caesarea Maritima in the east.

Caesarea! That's where everything changed for us. It was a fine place to be stationed. I was proud to be in command of some of the best of the Italian Cohort, men whose families had often come from Rome itself. We served and protected the procurators and prefects of the whole of Judaea and the city was constantly welcoming delegations from places like Jerusalem and Petra. I was headquartered not far from the magnificent harbor of Sebastos. I could stand on the steps and see the ships waiting to dock. Looking up along the beach I could see the mighty theater where the games and performances took place every fifth year. Perhaps that's why Ephesus held such appeal when the time came; that constant reminder the sea gives that there is a world awaiting exploration.

I was respected for my service, and everyone knew that I was trustworthy and fair in my dealings. Discipline sometimes called for harshness, but I hope I tempered it always with mercy. Fewer people, perhaps, knew where my faith was taking me. That was an even bigger adventure! And a dangerous one.

My connections with the faith of the Jews had started as fascination and had deepened into respect and commitment. I saw to it that they were treated properly if any came into contact with my men. I used my position to help when the synagogue needed repairs and as Jewish refugees arrived, having been forced to flee their homes in more hostile cities. I gave money to those in need and supported the Jewish community as they collected funds to help others. I loved their holy books and had friends who would help me to understand what I was reading. Their prayers became my prayers and their traditions wove themselves into the life of our home; our household altar was quietly dedicated to the God they worshipped. We chose our slaves with great care so that they did not gossip about our choices.

When Pilate returned from that Passover in Jerusalem I got the full reports. It was the first time I heard the name of Jesus. As the days followed, it became clear that this crucified rabbi was deeply divisive and challenging to my Jewish friends. Some were openly speaking about him as their long-awaited savior. Others took his crucifixion at the hands of Rome as ample proof that he could not be. Talk of resurrection was argued and debated and a host of theories were being picked over.

In all of this, my wife and I felt the terrible ambiguity of our position. Here I was, one of the leading officers Pilate had at his command, as Roman as could be, sitting with Jewish friends discussing the probability that a man some of my men had helped to execute was none other than the servant of God sent to free the Jews from Roman occupation. Little wonder that discussions grew tense and we all agreed that we needed a bit of time and space to think.

And it was in the space that the angel found me. It was around three in the afternoon when he appeared. I was dozing in the shade. So, a dream maybe. Or maybe more than a dream. I knew I heard the words. I'm used to orders given and orders obeyed and these were orders for me. I didn't hesitate. I called Manius and Decimus because I knew they could be trusted with my life. And I arranged for Marcus to go with them. A Roman guard would see them quickly and safely to Joppa with the minimum of awkward questions. I watched them leave, off to a seaside town to find two Simons and, perhaps, some answers. I gathered the family and told them of these things and the waiting began.

Three days later, they arrived. Our family was joined by some of the close friends who shared our commitments and our curiosity. When Decimus brought Simon Peter and his friends in, I knelt before him and everyone else followed my lead. We wanted to honor him and the work of God that had brought him to our home. We wanted to be found worthy, to get things right. But we didn't know how exactly, and we didn't know who it was we were meeting. We were making things up as best we could.

Peter quickly put us right and had us treating him as an equal. He was a messenger and no more than that. And this was strange already. As he pointed out, his presence in our home made him unclean. Yet, here he was. My friendship and affection for my Jewish friends had always meant no meetings in our home. I understood where the boundaries and limits lay between us, even as we shared so much. I was always the Roman centurion, and they were always subjects under the empire. Peter's arrival and his first step across our threshold hinted at revolution, a new world beginning.

I recounted my vision. He listened and a smile accompanied his nods. As I found out later when we talked it all through, I hadn't been the only one receiving visions and startling orders! And then he told us his story. It was the story of Jesus the teacher. It was the story of a Jewish fisherman and his friends and a Roman officer and his family. It was a story with a beginning, but not yet an ending. It was a story on its way, open and waiting for us to join in.

Peter told it with utmost simplicity. All he did was recount the events he had witnessed and how they had changed him. He trusted the story because within it he knew the hand of God. He spoke of the death of Jesus in ways no military report could ever manage. The Spirit of God was with Jesus throughout his life and work, and that work was always to bring blessing and hope to those in need and challenge and test to those in power. We had crucified him and God had raised him three days later. Peter had met him many times afterward, the nails still scarring him. Not a feeling or a phantom or the delusion of the grief-broken, but flesh and blood. And in his name, Peter and the others were being sent out from Jerusalem to tell the story and to assure all with ears to hear that forgiveness and salvation were the gifts God offers to all who believe.

Even before he finished speaking, we felt the change begin in us. Some were wiping quiet tears. Others were on their knees in prayer. Some stood, arms lifted high, swaying to a music only they could hear. Some were speaking in strange tongues. Some laughed; not the sneers of scorn but the ringing sound of sheer joy. I felt a sense of rightness, a sense of presence, a profound conviction that God accepted me just as I was.

Peter and those who had come with him were astounded. It turns out that God's revolution had to be as much in them as it was in us, Gentile and Jew equally blessed and equally caught up in the wonders of salvation. A new world being born. So much being undone and torn aside even as the newness rooted in our souls. We didn't know what baptism meant until Peter explained it. Then it seemed the perfect way to honor God's reality. We were all baptized.

They stayed and we talked and the little picture of Jesus grew as pieces were added to the mosaic in our minds. From then on, through the remainder of our time in Caesarea and now in Ephesus, we have no need of Roman gods of home and city and empire. This is the risk we gladly take, for we have the truth of who it is we worship when we light the lamps.

The Jailer of Paul and Silas

YES, I WILL TELL you all of it again. I suspect you will be as unwilling to
believe it this time as before. But you keep saying you want to know the
truth, and the truth is what I have to give. You trust me with the prisoners
you send. Why not trust me when I tell you how these prisoners ended up
being free? They could have watched me die then. Instead, they saved my
life. I am here to tell it because they refused to take what they might have
taken, refused to run when every door was hanging wide open. And they
refused to quietly slip away when their honor demanded more from us than
we wished to give. I know how much they have got under your skins, how
much their story haunts. Trust me, they got under my skin before they did
a thing to you!

Our prison in Philippi has seen many come and go and I have guarded
them for eleven years now. The cells can hold plenty, but we often keep
the inner ones waiting for the worst offenders. I've watched murderers and
deserters arrive with all the strutting confidence they could manage, only
to be dragged out weeks later to face trial and execution like frightened
kittens. The darkness and the damp get inside. The stink of bodies and the
smell of fear are choking in that hole.

The first I knew about Paul and Silas was when word came from the
magistrates. They were special prisoners who needed tight security. When
they arrived they were already a mess. They had been beaten and their
naked bodies were bloodied and bent. One of them could hardly put any
weight on his left leg. We shoved them into the hole and I locked the stocks
around their ankles. Already there was something unusual about them. I've
been called everything imaginable. I've been spat at and learned to duck
the kicks and lunges when we're putting on the ropes and chains. But these
two were quiet and compliant, not resisting at all. Not broken either, not

defeated. Just allowing us to do our job with no fuss or bother. And, as I walked away, they started singing to their god!

We set the watch and did the rounds of all the cells to check the place was secure for the night. I went upstairs and ate with my family.

It must have been about the third watch when the earthquake came. I've been in several before; including the massive one here in Philippi five years ago. The whole prison shook to its roots. I heard cracking as some of the timbers gave way and a whole chunk of wall fell into the courtyard. There were screams and shouts as people ran out of the buildings into the streets. I leapt down the stairs, not even thinking they might not be safe. I called Marius and we lit torches before we started checking the cells. What we saw!

The quake had been so strong that it had twisted iron and shattered wood and stone. It was as if the whole building had thrown itself to one side and all the cells lay open. Some had no doors left at all! Others had bars leaning so far out that a man could easily pass through the gap. One whole wall was just a heap on the ground. And every cell was empty! It was a mass escape triggered by the gods themselves.

"We're dead," Marius said, his voice flat. We both knew it. Dereliction of duty is one of the great crimes in the army. Guarding prisoners is at the heart of making sure justice is done. Letting them run away is a high crime, punishable in the most brutal way. The best we might do now was save a little honor for our families. I didn't need to be persuaded. I didn't even stop to say my goodbyes. Better for Silvana to think I died in the mayhem than see me put on trial, locked in the cells beneath her bed and executed one bright and sunny morning. Better for our children never to know the truth. I drew my sword.

"No!" rang a voice in the dark. "Everyone is here. None have escaped. Come and see."

We grabbed the torches and turned toward the hole. The flames reflected on dozens of pairs of eyes. The heart of the prison was crammed with every prisoner! Some were crouching on the floor, still chained together. Others stood as best they could, bending low to cope with the ceiling. And, in the midst of them all, Silas and Paul. Their stocks had burst open. They were as free as any of them. They all could have taken us down. But they hadn't. They were all doing the one thing it made no sense for them to do. They were quietly waiting to be locked up again.

I knelt in the muck and mess in front of our two most dangerous prisoners, and begged them to explain. Paul spoke of freedom, but not the freedom I expected. He spoke of following the way laid down by a god-man named Jesus. He told us of his life and death and how he had come back to life again. He told us of his own story; of his hatred of this savior and his followers and then his unbelievable conversion. "That had been my prison," he said. "And now I have a freedom none can take away." Silas joined in, completing the picture of their service and the wonders they had witnessed as the power and presence of this Jesus opened up the work of the God of the Jews. And now this Jewish God was receiving Gentiles, saving all who followed this way!

Marius, as startled as I, began leading the others back to their shattered cells and sorting guards to cover the remainder of the night. I took Paul and Silas upstairs to where Silvana and the children were waiting and worrying. It took time to explain! But then we poured water into the basins and I made the prisoners let us wash their wounds and soothe their cuts with ointment and oil. We found them clothes and gave them food. It seemed to be the right thing. Even the children ended up helping, their shyness forgotten.

Paul had spoken of baptism. It was a sign of taking on this way of faith, this journey into a new life with God. It was a rebirth. Of course, we knew we had so much to learn and so much to understand. Silvana worried that we might be in shock and not really thinking straight. "What if we bring trouble down upon us?" she wondered. We talked it through. We looked across at Paul and Silas. "Aren't they the proof we need?" I asked. "They have every reason to hate us, and yet they don't. They had every reason to escape and leave me to face the consequences, but they didn't. There is something in the way they are that I want for myself and for you and for us all; a peace and a trust. There is hope and life and joy here. Something so real. Something so good. More than we have ever known." She did feel it too. Much more than the earth was being shaken and rearranged that night.

In the end all of us were baptized, Paul speaking words of love and newness whilst Silas held the basin. As the rest of the night passed, we sat together and the two of them taught us many things about the journey we were just beginning.

And that is how we get to be where we are this morning. The magistrates sent for the prisoners with word of their freedom. Paul and Silas refused to be set free again! They claimed their Roman citizenship and knew their rights perfectly well. Their beating and imprisonment were illegal. All of you came to the prison then, worried and nervous. If news of this got to the wrong ears things could turn nasty. Apologies were made. Apologies were accepted. And my two new friends quietly went off. Only later did I discover that they spent time with Lydia, the cloth merchant. Only now have I found that she, too, is a follower of The Way.

The days have passed. Repairs continue. I still work the cells. But most of us who locked the gates that night, and many who were locked inside, have tasted a new kind of freedom. And it is very good.

Damaris, a Woman in Athens Who Heard Paul

WE GREW UP WITH the temples and banners on the Acropolis reaching for the gods. We have been carried as babies to be blessed by Athena and we have played hide and seek as children around the mighty columns of her temple. We have watched the smoke rising from so many altars and seen the clouds of white doves circling at dusk. The Acropolis speaks of who we are and of the gods who protect and nurture us. It speaks of ancient times; ages long gone as our people carved an empire and as our city gained its glory. It is always busy, bustling with pilgrims, worshippers, and the business of state. I can't remember a time when one of the temples wasn't hidden behind scaffolding and when the sound of chisels didn't ring against stones being repaired or prepared. The place is a magnet and a marvel.

My life had its rhythm and its security. Our family traces its origins far back and we have been part of the governance of Athens since at least the time of my great grandparents. I have taken my place in the processions up to the ancient citadel, singing with the choirs and wearing my best as the festivals begin. I have listened to the great decrees and watched as the magnificent moments of pageantry and politics have displayed. I take pride in my people and all we stand for. I understand the things that shape us and give us the strength and power admired across the empire. I know the glory of our craft and the beauty of our art. Few can turn stone into the likeness of flesh the way we can. No wonder the traders from Rome come seeking the best of our work. And little wonder that the best of all remains quietly here where it can be properly appreciated and honored. The gods have looked kindly upon us, and we worship them with every gift and skill we can conjure.

That was me. That was what I inherited and all I drew upon to shape my life and fashion my future. But the stones of the Acropolis are not the only theater for Athens. Stand with your back to the Parthenon and look down to the northwest and you see a vast bare block of bleached stone standing above the cedars, large enough for a crowd to gather. In earlier days, councils met upon the Hill of Ares to rule on many things. That still happens on occasion, but the Areopagus is more often used as a place to gather and debate. It has become our greatest public classroom. And it was here that my life was turned.

The followers of The Way were already known about in Athens before Paul reached us. Their strange ways and their stranger stories became the stuff of gossip when travelers passed through. We hosted several in our home who spoke of works of wonder, the miraculous doings of wandering teachers and seekers. They told the tale of the Jewish holy man named Jesus who had died on a Roman cross only to come back to life three days later. His name had the power, so the stories went, to heal the sick and make followers from the most mighty to the most vulnerable. His communities were becoming places where the sharing and belonging went deep. Existing loyalties and duties were being overturned. His followers were meeting plenty of anger and suspicion; some had given up their lives for him. All this was already in the air when word came of the arrival of Paul of Tarsus. His reputation intrigued many of us. His wanderings had stirred trouble and shaped no few lives around the empire. It came as little surprise to hear that he was soon caught up in argument in the synagogue and argument in the marketplace. He agreed to debate at the Areopagus and many of us crowded in to listen.

I was standing with some of my family when Paul began. The Acropolis stood in the background, gleaming in early afternoon sunshine. The smoke was rising straight up and the banners were not moving. There was no breeze at all. We settled under the awnings to find some shade and fanned ourselves as the heat grew and hung heavy.

Paul began to speak. I've held a stage myself and listened to much oratory. I know the tricks and skills and ways of weaving words to shape pictures in the minds of a crowd and to play their mood. I know how to persuade and how to repel. I've felt myself carried to the heights and plunging the depths as the words have worked their magic.

So, I knew what he was doing as Paul started with flattery. He was the humble visitor taking in the city sights, browsing our wares, appreciating

our culture. I had never found an altar to an unknown god but could perfectly well imagine such a one was waiting to be noticed. I knew enough
about Jewish thought to recognize Paul taking us to their creation stories;
to Adam shaped by the god they name as the only god. The contrast with all
we believed about the gods and goddesses bringing everything into being
was stark. Stark, but not surprising. Neither was Paul's tilting against our
worship and our temples a shock. I remember a few of us smiling together
that he was using one of our own altars to tell us that our altars were empty
of meaning and power. No harm in hitting us with a little irony!

I was starting to think of slipping away. There didn't, after all seem
to be much new here. Several of us whispered that we couldn't see what
the fuss was about or why this man was such a cause of trouble. He wasn't
offering anything to change the world. Until he did.

It was his image of us groping for the gods that made me pause. I loved
that image the moment I heard it. And then, of course, I realized that he
was not speaking of our gods any more. He wasn't interested in Athena and
Chaos, he wasn't speaking of the powers of Gaea and Eros or the mysteries
of Erebus and Nyx. He didn't wonder how Nemesis might shape and starve
and bless our lives. He was standing in the shadow of the Acropolis and saw
me groping in the shadows of my mind and of my faith. He was speaking of
the god he knew, the god whose power and purpose he was convinced we
needed. He was talking to me of the god I needed to know.

I was listening now, whispering no longer. Paul began to unfold the
truth he wanted us to hear, and it was as if in all that crowd his audience was
only me. He named me as a child of the god he worshipped. This god knew
me. Not as a distant power at work in everything, needing proper homage
and sometimes fickle. The god Paul worshipped was a lover of intimacy, a
creator whose delight was in drawing closer and closer to all that had shape
and form and life. Paul's god knew me in my longings and in my sadness as
much as in my devotion and certainty. And this god had come to find me.
More. This god had come to live amongst us, had died our death, and had
risen from the dead to assure us of his power and his welcome. In his name,
we all could be made new.

I knew the arguments that I could make. I was a proud and happy
Athenian. I did not need this god that Paul had come to sell. For generations we had crafted our altars and carved our gods, and our lives were
rich and full and good. But, what if all this time my worship had hidden a
secret? What if there was a longing that no sacrifice could satisfy? What if

Paul had come to show me how to find my way home before I even knew that I was lost? What if there was a truth older than any temple on our hills waiting to be found?

Scripture Index

SCRIPTURE INDEX

Index of Seasons of the Christian Year
(using the Revised Common Lectionary)